The Island

The Island

DAVID BOROFKA

MacMurray & Beck
Denver/Aspen

Earlier versions of the following chapters have appeared as listed:
"An Introduction to Old Friends" in *Black Warrior Review*
(Fall/Winter 1995); "How You Are Born" in *The Missouri Review*
(Winter 1996); "The Defenestration of Dubček's Hat" in *Great River
Review* (Spring 1997); "A Train Heading South" in *The Gettysburg
Review* (Spring 1997); and "Adagio, 1958" in
Shenandoah (Winter 1996).

Printed and bound in the United States of America

1   2   3   4   5   6   7   8   9   10

Library of Congress Cataloging-in-Publication Data
Borofka, David, 1954–
The island : a novel / by David Borofka.
p.   cm.
ISBN 1–878448–78–1
I. Title.
PS3552.075443I85   1997
813'.54—dc21   97–20583
CIP

MacMurray & Beck Fiction; General Editor, Greg Michalson
The Island cover design by Laurie Dolphin,
interior design by Stacia Schaefer.
The text was set in Weiss by Lyn Chaffee.

For Robert and Martha Borofka

1

AN
INTRODUCTION
TO
OLD
FRIENDS

When I was fourteen, my father and I were at Chavez Ravine in the lower deck behind third base. The Dodgers had fallen behind 8-1 to the Cardinals, and by the fifth inning most of the crowd had drifted away, looking for other distractions. Three rows down one of the vendors sank into an empty seat, his hat pulled low over his forehead, the tray spread across his lap. The palm trees behind the outfield bleachers drooped in the haze of early evening. Even the players seemed dispirited and preoccupied, moving as though they were figures in a dreamscape. Then, as the count reached 0-and-2 on Willie Davis, my father announced that he and my mother would be spending the summer in Germany in lieu of a divorce.

"Look, it's not the end of the world. This is a good thing, this trip," he said, clapping me on the shoulder. He must have thought the gesture fatherly because he suddenly began recounting episodes from early childhood, his as well as mine: first girlfriends, fistfights in school, narrow escapes from injury or punishment, that sort of thing. In the sixth grade he had once danced with a one-legged girl. They waltzed, and the thump of her wooden leg on the floor was as regular as a metronome. When I was three, I fell into a koi pond. By the time my father pulled me out, my eyes were bulging in their sockets like a carp's, and I've gone by the name Fish ever since. Etcetera, etcetera. These recollections brought a flush to his cheeks that half a dozen beers had failed to produce, and I wondered about the strange misdirections our pursuits of happiness often take.

The direction I would be taking—at least for the summer—was north to Oregon and the home of my father's best friend in grade school, Miles Lambert. His children, Freddy and Mira, sixteen and fourteen, respectively, were as near to me in age as I could possibly want; when I was four years old I had played with them during one of our rare vacation trips, but I could not recall a single memory. My father, on the other hand, could go way back. When Miles Lambert and he were in second grade, their teacher, an old maid named Miss Florio, had disciplined the boys by making them crouch in the kneehole of her desk, their faces anchored between her thighs, and when they were released, their cheeks were printed with the outline of her garters.

"I wish I were going with you, Fish. See old Miles. The jolly lager drinkers will be interesting for only so long, and then your mother will start firing up the credit cards. I have to believe somebody's going to be having a good time, and it might as well be you."

"Might as well," I said.

The way he described it, Miles Lambert's house was a private country club without the dress code, a brick Tudor mansion inherited from his wife's grandfather, who had owned a shipyard during World War II. A swimming pool that dated from the jazz age. Tennis courts. A squash court. Hills and creeks and trees.

"It's a goddamn paradise. You'll have to remind yourself that it's just a temporary thing. We'll leave in June, come back in August, and you'll be screaming you don't want to leave. But we'll know what we're going to do then. It's not as though we weren't coming back, and I bet we'll be together when we do."

I hadn't assumed otherwise, but once voiced, the various and unfortunate possibilities seemed altogether real no matter how Edenic the Lambert estate. At that moment Tim McCarver unloaded a double into the deep reaches of left-center, another thousand people rose from their seats, and I noticed the spot on my father's jaw he had missed while shaving that morning. "We'll be hashing things out," my father said, "while you're having the time of your life."

My parents' usual solution to their marital problems involved spending great sums of money. The sofa in the living room, my mother's car, the Italian tile in the entryway were all testimony to various quarrels. In other words, my parents had done this before, but never at so great a distance. Their last argument had occasioned a trip to San Francisco, a mere six hours away, and they had come back a day later with an Oriental carpet sticking out the back of their Suburban like a load of lumber. By those appliances and elements of decor that appeared as if by magic, I could read the signs of my parents' disaffection. In the code of my parents' marriage, however, I wasn't sure what a trip to Germany meant.

My mother had not come with us to the baseball game. "Not my meat, Buster," she had said, but she had not expected my father to spill the beans about their trip in the middle of Dodger Stadium either. "Your father ought to have his head examined," she said later that night. She sat on the edge of my bed, still dressed for the bishop's tea she had attended instead of the ball game. My mother had long ago decided that Episcopalianism was a classier activity than either bridge or bowling. A better brand of people. "We were going to take you to dinner, give you the whole setup in stages." She patted my arm with the same motion she used for our cats, and I caught the fading scent of her perfume, cigarette smoke, and the social niceties of small talk among polite company. "Give your father a beer and he turns into Louella Parsons."

"I don't mind," I said.

"Yeah, well, you ought to."

"When do you go?"

She sighed. "Soon. Two weeks."

"Are you looking forward to it?"

She shifted in her spot on the bed, crossed then uncrossed her legs, rested her chin in her hands, her elbows on her knees. Light, reflected from the hallway, traced her cheek, a curl of her hair, the pearls warming at her throat. "Well, a summer in Germany sounds fun, doesn't it?"

"I guess so. I'm going to Oregon."

"I know. Your father and I need some serious time together, and you'd just be bored with us."

I would have liked to tell her that I would be happy to be bored with them so long as they were together. If they wanted to sit in a *Biergarten* all day long to settle things, I could take along books or I could watch television in the hotel room. I wanted to tell her that they couldn't make such decisions without me, that if they shipped me off their decision would be made already, that of all their acquisitions I was the most important one, the one reminder that happiness could last.

How to explain my parents? My father was an investment banker, a drinker, and an optimist, not necessarily in that order. He loved all racquet sports; he played tennis and squash religiously. He had gone to good schools, he chose the right friends, and he knew the advantages of the Windsor knot over the simple four-in-hand. His one inexplicable act was marrying my mother, who was, at the time, Miles Lambert's fiancée. My mother was a seamstress who had quit school at the end of her eighth grade year. She apprenticed with a men's clothier and fell in love with every forty-two regular under thirty years of age. She met Miles Lambert in the shop when he was searching for a thirty-eight extra long, and although she could do nothing for his clothing needs, she was engaged to him two months later. Only to marry my father, Mr. Lambert's best friend. Miles Lambert was stationed in the South Pacific, and my father had taken to dropping in at the men's store where she worked.

In his version of the story she marked some slacks for alteration, and it became an epiphany of love and chemistry. She had strong fingers and a mouthful of pins, and they suffered a delicate moment when she gauged his inseam. My father knew that such a prickly woman could provide what he needed. According to my mother, however, my father, for reasons she could not possibly fathom, pursued her with an aggressiveness that bordered on the obsessive. He took her to the movies, to dances, and to dinner. He bought her things, the more expensive the better. What was truth and what fiction, my parents wouldn't tell, and they both stuck to their stories.

What they could agree to was the fact that my mother was not my father's equal socially; she made up for her educational shortcomings by close observation. They also agreed, quite readily, that they had almost nothing in common; they could barely talk to one another, so divergent were their past experiences. Such differences and the resulting confusions were often the source of argument. They argued about my father's drinking, my mother's diction, and their respective flirtations and improprieties. They argued about who had betrayed Miles Lambert.

The odd thing was that they never quarreled about money. They found much to argue about, my parents did, but they never haggled over each other's material desires, for that may have been the one thing each respected in the other.

Two days after school let out my parents put me on a plane to Portland. When my boarding call was announced, my father handed me an envelope, then pulled me to his chest. My mother held her purse in both hands. "Got everything?"

"I think so."

"Call us when you get to Miles's place," my father said.

"All right."

"And don't go running off with any good-looking women," my father said. "Airplanes are full of them."

"That's *your* problem, Alan," my mother said. "Let the boy alone, why don't you?"

"Your mother—"

"Bye," I said, edging toward the jetway. "I'll call you tonight."

I left them still arguing about my father's supposed infidelities. It was an argument without much spirit, old ground they had covered many, many times, and I suppose even they had grown tired of it. When I looked back one last time, my father was listening to my mother's continuing reproach, his ear to her mouth, as though she were whispering endearments.

The envelope my father had given me contained two hundred dollars, spending money for the summer. "Don't get into a poker game with Miles," my father wrote in the note paper-clipped to the twenties, "or Freddy. Especially Freddy, since he won't give the money back."

Once belted into my seat, I couldn't help checking, rechecking, my pocket, making sure that the money was still there. I was certain that a hole would open up and the money would be lost before the plane reached Portland. I would enter the terminal and there would be no one to meet me, all the money would be gone, and I would be a thousand miles from home without the means to call. And what if my parents had decided to leave for Europe early without telling me? I would be lost and without hope.

Or I might get to Portland only to find out that Miles Lambert, though my father's friend, was a tyrant who hated other people's children. I had friends at school who told stories about their own parents; pleasant enough in public, but in the privacy of their own homes they became ill-tempered monsters.

Through the window I could see the ground crew below the wing. They were laughing as they waited. For what? They were inspecting something on the underside of the wing, and their chins were pointed up. What did they know that was so funny? I suddenly imagined the airplane—thousands of feet in the air, a mere toy to those below—breaking apart and bodies falling from the sky like an entire species of failure, *Homo icarus*.

The overhead compartment suddenly seemed too low, the seats too narrow, the rows too close together. The air was stuffy and close.

"I can't do this," I said.

The blue-haired woman in the aisle seat looked up from her Barbara Cartland but said nothing as I moved past the vacant middle seat and then her knees into the aisle.

"Excuse me, please. I'm sorry. Excuse me."

I walked up and down the aisle, standing for a time by the galley in the back by the smoking section, moving out of the way of the stewardesses, who were busily stowing away their supplies.

"You can't stay here too much longer," one of them said at last.

"I know." I think I was on the verge of marching back to the door, demanding to be let out. I could cash in my ticket and with that and the two hundred dollars rent a cheap motel room until my parents left for Germany; I could live by myself at home. Anything was preferable to this.

"I'll take you back to your seat now," the stewardess said. "We're almost ready to go."

"I can't seem to get any air," I said. "I can't breathe. I feel like I'm swimming in mud."

"It's a common reaction. Many people feel that way. Even experienced fliers."

"But I can't breathe."

"There, there." She was gentle and quiet, this stewardess, very calm. She had the pale features of an English lady-in-waiting, and her short blond hair seemed designed to accentuate her own relative youth and innocence. "There, now," she said, "you'll be fine. I'm sure of it."

We stood next to my row, where I saw for the first time that the vacant middle seat was now occupied by a girl not many years older than I but clearly in the latter stages of pregnancy. She shifted in her seat and groaned when she realized she would have to get up and move out into the aisle in order to let me through.

"I'm sorry, really. I didn't mean to cause trouble."

"Of course you didn't," said the stewardess.

"Oh, golly," the pregnant girl said. "If my water breaks, this will be a most unhappy flight."

"There's no need of that, dear," the blue-haired lady said. "I think this young man will stay put, won't you?"

"Of course," I said. "I'm done wandering."

I wasn't entirely certain. The overhead compartment still seemed awfully low, but simple courtesy and good manners would keep me in my seat, overcome my qualms, especially in such close proximity to someone ready to eject a baby at the slightest joggle.

The girl's name was Donna; she was flying against doctor's orders, but she was bound and determined to get home. Her father had sent her the ticket. She was from Portland originally, but her soldier-boyfriend had brought her to San Francisco before he left for Vietnam, and she had then migrated to Los Angeles by herself looking for work at the studios before she realized she was pregnant. Now, however, she was flying home to have the baby because her boyfriend had written that he no longer loved her, he didn't think he had ever loved her—she had tricked him at a moment when he had been vulnerable. She had not told him about the baby and now she couldn't possibly.

"I'm so sorry, dear," the blue-haired lady said, patting her on one arm. "These things happen, terrible as they are. Personally, I never married, although I had my opportunities. The right man never came to my door, and I've lived with loneliness for thirty-five years as a result."

The irony, Donna said, was that the next day she got the phone call she'd been dreading for six months: her boyfriend's father saying that her boyfriend wouldn't be coming home, that he'd been killed in a mortar attack. She had screamed and cried over the phone, but that was partly an act, she realized now. Part of her was glad that the son of a bitch had gotten what he deserved, but how could you say that over the phone to the dead boy's father?

The blue-haired lady, whose name was Mary Rochelle Dunbar, listed her own methods for dealing with loneliness. She had travelled to Italy and France. She had a nursing degree and provided services to the poor. Her family had provided her with an income, and she supposed she should be thankful that she hadn't needed to support a husband, as had certain friends of hers. They had settled for something far less than the best, and they were not so happy now.

We had taken off heading out over the ocean, and the bright blue of the Pacific seemed cheery and hopeful, in stark contrast to the dull browns and grays of the dry, industry-littered coast. Miss Dunbar was dozing again over her romance. Donna had tilted her seat back, and her eyes were closed against the afternoon sun streaming through the window. When I lowered the blind, her eyelids fluttered open. "Mmm. Thanks."

Pregnancy had not treated her well. The skin of her face was mottled and puffy, whiskers covered her chin, her wrists were swollen, and her fingers looked as though they were all knuckle. There were no laces in her running shoes, and she wore them like slip-ons.

"What he did was horrible," I said. "You should have told him about the baby."

"Who? You mean my dead boyfriend?" She leaned closer to me after first glancing in Miss Dunbar's direction. "That was just a gag. I don't even know who the father is, maybe my boyfriend the dope fiend, maybe the guy in the apartment next door or that little twerp in my anthro class, maybe the chaplain. Who knows? It's a funny thing: free love is fine so long as it's with a dead war hero who turns out to be a stump. Otherwise, forget it. You're just a slut." She settled back into her pillow and closed her eyes again, her hands resting on the mound of her belly. "It's a beautiful story, though, isn't it? The rejection of true love."

"My parents are sending me to live with friends," I said, "so they can go to Germany, spend a lot of money, and get divorced anyway."

One eye opened, but she was shaking her head. "Nice try, Gonzo, but a little too exotic. The more common the better. Not Germany. Lake Tahoe I could accept. Niagara Falls maybe, just maybe. Germany is too far and too arbitrary. Who would go to Germany to save a troubled marriage? Adolf and little Eva?"

"Good point."

"Try again."

"I'm going to visit my grandmother."

She ground the heels of her hands into her eyes. "I believe it," she groaned, "but it's shit-brown boring. A story has to have a little pizzazz, after all. If you can't tell an interesting lie, you might as well forget it."

Thirty minutes from our scheduled arrival time in Portland, Donna nudged my arm, a sly smile creasing her face. Below us clouds massed like mountains. "Should we see if we can get home a little faster?" she whispered.

"What are you going to do," I asked, "take over the plane?"

"Watch."

She began groaning then, as if there were screams caught in the back of her throat. Her hand gripped my arm.

"Hey," I said, "that hurts."

"Aah, aah, oww-w-w."

The older woman's head snapped up. "What? What is it?"

"I don't know," I said. "Something's wrong."

"Get someone," Donna gasped. "Please, oh, hurry." She began breathing through her mouth like a runner in the last stage of collapse. "Goddamn it," she screamed, but as her head went from side to side, she winked at me.

Miss Dunbar reached forward to press the call button, and two stewardesses came running. "What's the matter, sweetheart?" said the one who had helped me back to my seat. "Is the baby starting to come?"

"I think so."

The other stewardess ran toward first class, and then I heard the suction of the cockpit door opening and closing again. Only a moment later, it seemed as though the noise of the jet engines were pitched a key higher.

"See?" Donna mouthed to me. "What did I tell you?"

But then I thought someone surely must have spilled a drink under our seats. I heard the sound of a sudden, momentary downpour, then something dripping, and instead of relaxing her hold on my arm, she dug her fingers in even further, her nails drawing blood.

"No," she said. "Fucking son of a bitch. No."

"Let go." I tried to pry her fingers from my arm, but they seemed to be locked in place. "Enough," I said.

"Babies don't wait, young man," Miss Dunbar said. "They come when it's most inconvenient. Always." She was rolling up the sleeves of her blouse. "I'd look out the window if I were you. You don't want to watch this."

The baby was halfway out as the plane landed, and Miss Dunbar was a local celebrity by that evening's newscast. The baby wasn't quite turned at first, so she and Donna had their hands full, figuratively speaking. The baby, a girl, was born in Row 12, seat C. Donna's head was in my lap, and Miss Dunbar was squatting in the aisle issuing directives of when to push, when to breathe, and so on. As efficient as were the pilot, the crew, and the emergency personnel, Miss Dunbar was even more so. She waved the EMTs away while she finished with Donna, and by the time they had loaded Donna and the baby onto the gurney, Miss Dunbar had her hands washed, her makeup freshened, and her hair rearranged, which was quite a good thing since there were two news crews waiting for her at the gate. I was a wreck; during the whole ordeal I had looked away only to have my eyes drawn back time and again to Donna's bent knees and the bloody towels that seemed to be everywhere. Her screams were my screams. Why would anyone endure such a violent and nasty experience? The baby squalled, then looked at everyone with knowing eyes. Miss Dunbar handed her to the EMTs, who cleaned her up and handed the tidy bundle back to Donna. Under the blue ambulance blankets, Donna was so pale as to be transparent. The rest of us stared, only gradually becoming aware of the rain pattering on the windows like a signal releasing us back to the world.

Our departure was as orderly as a recessional: first the gurney—Donna, the baby, and the EMTs—then Miss Dunbar, and then the rest of us, quiet as though under a spell, no one making a mad dash for the overhead compartments or pushing ahead in the aisles, each passenger one part of an elaborate exercise of silent courtesy.

Through the gate and onto the concourse. Donna and her baby were already long gone, bound for St. Vincent's. I was suddenly aware that I didn't know what Miles Lambert looked like; I had seen pictures, of course, but try as I might all I could recall were the dim, generic features one might see in police sketches, and I was turning in slow circles with this unhappy realization. I could have looked at him twice and it still would have done me no good.

Down to baggage claim, where I waited for my father's old black leather monster. Bag after bag—suitcase, hatbox, and attaché—flopped onto the turnstiles as they went around and around, but mine was not among them, my private fears growing by leaps and bounds. I checked my pocket for the fifth time in as many minutes, reassured by the continuing presence of my father's envelope. At last, at the top of the conveyor belt, a battered black leather suitcase tilted forward, its saddle buckles cinched tight against theft or mishap, and as I reached to grab it, a hand clamped down on my shoulder, a voice murmuring like the grumble of distant thunder, "There you are."

I turned to face Miles Lambert. *How could I have forgotten such a man?* He appeared to me as a genial Ichabod Crane, all knobs and angles, elbows, knees, and shoulders. His Adam's apple danced above a collar at least two inches too large. His hair was white, his complexion pink. He seemed decades older than my father, and yet they had been schoolboy chums, and for a time they had lived together in college. It was the first insight I had that no matter how similar in sensibility and temperament, people age differently when they are apart.

"You slipped past me at the gate," Miles Lambert was saying. "You nearly escaped."

"Hello, Mr. Lambert," I said, shaking his large hand. His fingers could have wrapped around my own twice. "Thanks for meeting me."

"You must have thought you were on your own, is that it?" His great bushy eyebrows rose. "No matter. Mira's waiting in the car, Freddy's chasing around the countryside, I expect. You'll have a good summer while your folks are away."

I hurried to keep up with his long, loping strides.

"So. Your parents are well?"

"They're great," I said. "Terrific."

"Ah, ha. And you had an interesting flight, I understand."

"It was pretty weird," I said. "Some exciting moments though."

"I saw the news reporters and the medical people. You'll have to tell us all about it during dinner tonight."

He stopped abruptly in front of the automatic doors. "Look," he said, "look at it rain."

It was true. The light rain that had been falling during our landing had turned into a torrent. Water slid along the curbs. In the parking lots, umbrellas of every color bobbed between the roofs of the cars. Miles Lambert stepped on the floor pad with a ceremonial flourish, and the doors jerked open. The gesture was ironic as well as proprietary, as if he could command doors to open, the rain to fall. As if one could possibly believe such a thing. We made a dash for his car, a tired twenty-year-old Buick, the windows opaque with steam. Mr. Lambert deposited my suitcase in its cave of a trunk.

"I'd have you sit up front, but it's full of junk," he said. The passenger side, both seat and floor, was full of boxes with cable and wire of various descriptions struggling to escape.

"You can sit in the back with Mira. She won't bite. Will you, Peanut?"

"Stop it, Daddy."

A girl with glasses unfolded long legs from underneath herself as she set a paperback beside her on the seat. Her hair was damp as though she had just come from a shower, which must have been the source of the condensation on the windows.

"This is my daughter, Mira. I don't guess you remember playing together the last time you were here."

"No."

"Mira, say hello to Fish."

"Hi," she yawned.

"Hi."

I got into the seat behind Mr. Lambert's.

Mira draped her arms over the back of the front seat, shifting one of the boxes so her head could poke through. "Can we go to Sauvie Island before we go home?"

"Are you kidding me?" Mr. Lambert aimed the Buick toward the booths at the edge of the lot. "It's a deluge out there, little girl. She wants," he said, looking at me in the rearview mirror, "to pick strawberries. We'd be up to our shins in mud."

"Oh, Daddy. Fish doesn't mind, do you?" she said, turning to me.

As fourteen-year-old girls go, she was not particularly pretty, but it was already evident that sometime in the near future she would become gorgeous, overtaking all those other girls who never know a moment's uncertainty, conventionally attractive from one day to the next. Her glasses would one day be lost, her hair would thicken and become glossy, her features would go from awkward to striking. She would grow into her nose. She seemed to take for granted that the future would be hers; my acquiescence would only confirm what she already knew. Waiting for my answer, she picked up her book, a dog-eared copy of something called *The Secret Doctrine.*

"No," I said, "I don't mind. It's fine with me." My tongue felt like a block of wood, and my limbs had become clumsy, self-conscious. My stomach turned over, and I wondered if my father had felt like this the day he had gotten a pair of trousers altered.

"Don't let her bully you," Mr. Lambert said. "You let her start, there'll be no end to it. I ought to know."

"Daddy."

"It's her mother's fault."

Something in their respective tones suggested that this was a game they had played many times before, a game in which each player understood the other's movements perfectly, and as a spectator I was invited to watch and admire. But any other participation was not required.

Rain beat on the Buick's roof in an even higher pitch. The wipers flapped back and forth as they struggled to sweep the water away. Mr. Lambert began to tell a story about his wife, whom he had met while he was stationed on Samoa. Ariana gave orders all the time: she had once marched him outside into the teeth of a cyclone, and now she was raising their daughter in her own image.

"I'm warning you, Fish," Mr. Lambert said, "since you look like a decent sort of guy. You get mixed up with Lambert women, you better be ready to take on the tigers."

"Don't embarrass me," Mira said.

"What? How could I embarrass you? What did I say? I ask you, Fish, what did I say?"

I sank back into the Buick's couch of a back seat. I shook my head in answer to Mr. Lambert, feeling as though I too were a newborn, viewed for the first time by my discoverers, ready to be taken to a home I'd never seen, only dreamed of.

"I'm asking you, Fish. Did you hear anything wrong?"

"Nothing," I said. "I didn't hear a thing."

2

HOW
YOU
ARE
BORN

Miranda Lambert's bedroom was on the third floor of the family's manor house, overlooking the sweep of the back lawn, the reflecting pool, the twin gazebos, and the rose garden. During the winter, Mira said, the view was not remarkable; mist obscured the details of the scene like a painting that has been overworked, and clouds provided such a low ceiling as to make a submariner claustrophobic. In winter the drapes were rarely opened, but in summer, during those moments when the overcast was suspended, the picture from her leaded glass windows was something out of a fairy tale, including the beauties of the back half of the estate as well as the Olympian triangle of Mount Hood.

Today the drapes were open, but she was not admiring the landscape. She was, instead, trying to teach me the intricacies of a card game called hell bridge. With little success, I might add. It was some variation of rummy or Michigan kitty that the Lambert family played, but Mira was not a normal girl, and her explanation of the rules sounded like something out of Lewis Carroll. I could make no sense of it.

"You're not trying, Fish," she said, the hollows below her cheeks growing red with exasperation. "This isn't geometry or logarithms."

"I know it's not." I stifled a yawn. "Freddy had me up all night."

The night before, at midnight, her brother had shaken me out of a fitful and restless sleep to invite me to a party down by the river. He opened the window of my room and showed me the way across the slate roof and down the trellis on the south side of the house to the ground. Freddy was two years older and had recently obtained his driver's license, and I was flattered that he would include me. Only later did I realize that he had invited me because my bedroom window was his only escape route.

Our way was lighted by a fickle moon that played tag with the clouds. At one moment the path along the roof was outlined as clearly as day; the next we were feeling our way toward the edge, where nothing separated the roof from the ground but air. Then down the trellis, clutching the ivy, and across the back lawn, sprinting like burglars from one shadowed border to the other.

"No, no, no," Mira was saying, "a run of four has to be in the same suit."

"You said they had to be in sequence."

"*And* in the same suit," she huffed. "Honestly, Fish."

"Don't be snotty."

"Don't be stupid."

I swallowed one more enormous yawn, then stretched out on the braided rug. Although her bedroom was large and elevated, the only habitable room on the third floor, it was not a fourteen-year-old girl's pink-and-cream fantasy. The wallpaper was peeling off plaster walls that were themselves crumbling, wind whistled through the casements and down the chimney of her fireplace, and a person could easily pick up splinters from the hardwood floor. In the center of an ornate rose medallion, an unshaded bulb dangled from an archaic wire. By comparison, on the floor below, the room that I was assigned had been completely redone: paint, floors, fixtures, the works.

Mira's mother had told me that her daughter's room was the last of the Lambert house to be renovated. Mira had so far frustrated her mother's efforts, saying she liked her room as it was, but Mrs. Lambert was closing in. I was reminded of my father's aunt: near the end of her days she became convinced that the nuclear threat was imminent and, claiming that her twenty-three-room house was too big a target, chose to live in the detached garage. Mira's stubbornness seemed no less eccentric than my great-aunt's fright.

"This place is a dump," I said. "You ought to let your mother fix it."

"My mother isn't going to get within ten feet of this room." Mira held the deck of cards in her right hand, flexing them in the direction of my head. "Can you keep a secret?"

"I guess so. Sure."

"My mother is not going to touch this room because Claudia Montoya-Jones once spent the night here, and it was the most memorable night of my life. So far, that is."

The story of Claudia Montoya-Jones, at least as Mira told it, covered four decades, and it seemed to take that long in the telling. Mr. Lambert's first cousin once removed, Claudia Montoya-Jones was an extra in several movies in the 1920s. After the stock market crash, she declared herself a spiritual adviser, and in the '30s, '40s, and '50s she supported herself by offering a variety of services. Her preferred method for contacting the spirits was deep reverie. She also used tarot cards and a Ouija board, but these she dismissed as mere devices. Props for the uninitiated. As an actress she could not have convinced anyone that she was alive, much less become a character. But as a medium she had a faithful following; there were half a dozen producers who swore they would never make another movie without first consulting her. Vivien Leigh thought she was swell. She was married four times, each time to an older man who died within two years of the wedding. She did all right for herself. She corresponded with Edgar Cayce for six months until his death. But when she died in 1964 she was alone except for her contacts with the spirit world. A short while before her passing she visited Mira's father; she ate dinner with the family, told stories about Selznick and Goldwyn, and then long after midnight climbed the stairs to the room on the third floor. Mira was ten years old and supposed to be in bed, but she knocked on the door anyway. Madame Claudia showed Mira various mementos that she supposed would interest a child: a lock of Clark Gable's hair; a picture of herself and Orson Welles; a note from Bette Davis.

"I sat at her feet, but I couldn't think of a thing to say that wouldn't sound stupid and childish. I don't know what I expected. She began to whisper, saying that what she was about to tell me was to be kept in the strictest confidence, that my parents would be furious with her if they ever found out. She talked about astral projection, the transmigration of souls, Madame Blavatsky, reincarnation, theosophy, immortality. She showed me a necklace of crystals. It was a present to me, she said, but I'd have to wait until she was gone before I could collect it. It would be hidden somewhere in this room, and I'd

have to let the crystals call to me. Not five minutes after she
left, I was turning the room upside down. The boxsprings of
the bed, behind the pictures on the walls, the lampshades.
Nothing. I closed my eyes, and a little while later I felt an impression of heat coming from the fireplace. That's where I
found the necklace, wedged above the door of the flue. She
also left me her Ouija board and pointer, which I found in the
nightstand next to the bed even though I had checked there
once before for the necklace. Whether she meant to leave the
Ouija board, I don't know. I couldn't ask my parents. I
promised my silence, and I've kept my promise until now.
This room is saturated with the soul of Claudia Montoya-
Jones, and I refuse to lose her presence just because of some
stupid remodeling. My mother gets angry whenever we talk
about it, and Daddy feels guilty about crossing her.

"See," she said, holding what looked like dime-store jew-
elry in one hand and a battered box in the other. "You don't
believe me."

"I didn't say that." I was yawning, and I couldn't stop. "I
told you, I'm tired."

She bit her lip and seemed about to cry. "I have to show
you something tonight. I'll meet you in your room at nine o'-
clock," she said. "I know that's how you and Freddy get out of
the house—your window. I saw you last night. You looked
like a couple of apes running across the lawn. But don't worry.
I won't say a word to Mom or Dad."

Freddy had warned me that his sister was weird, but I truly
wasn't prepared for the degree to which that weirdness might
run. I honestly hadn't given it much thought. The night
before, after we had made our escape from the house, I had

followed Freddy through the back gardens and down an overgrown path that crossed the highway before terminating at the river. There were four others waiting for us on the ribbon of sand they called a beach, a small fire already burning. Freddy made the introductions: Duncan Rhodes and Sheila Baird, Sheila's sister, Amanda, and Gale Lewis.

"Fish Becker," Freddy said. "He's staying with us this summer."

"I suppose there's a story behind your name," Gale Lewis said. A dark-eyed girl as soft featured as a pillow, she snuggled up to Freddy. Her lips curved in what I could only think of as a proprietary gesture.

"Yeah," Freddy said, "but it's stupid."

Two bottles of bourbon, lifted from Duncan Rhodes's parents' liquor cabinet, began to make the rounds, and I took my turn. Sheila and Duncan told the story of how they had managed to sneak the bottles out of the house even though Duncan's father was home and drinking from the opened one at the time. It had been quite a clandestine operation, and they laughed so hard tears squeezed from Sheila's eyes as they told of hearing Duncan's father flailing around his study. "I could hear him turning over chairs," Duncan said. "And he was roaring at my mother, 'Margaret, the goddamn whiskey disappeared again.' I would have preferred gin, but it was worth it to hear the old man go on." Sheila's sister, Amanda— who had obviously been brought along as my date for the evening—took an exceptionally large gulp, choked, coughed, then giggled: a light falsetto that ended in an embarrassing snort, which the others pretended not to hear. Not long after the first bottle was finished, Freddy and Gale left to take a walk, and then Sheila and Duncan also stood up, saying they felt the need of some exercise. They staggered a bit getting to their feet, and moments later we heard them moving off into the quack grass. Then there was the sound of a belt buckle and the rustle of clothing, and Amanda began to un-button her plaid flannel shirt as if she had heard a signal. She had accompanied her sister on outings before.

"You can kiss me and touch me, but nothing further," she said.

"Oh."

In Los Angeles the girls who had consented to go with me to football games or dances had been remarkably aggres-sive kissers but extremely reluctant to abandon any article of clothing; by their conversation one might have imagined that they had night jobs, yet they always made sure to have breath mints handy and they always kept a sharp watch on the clock and the time when they would go home to their parents and the security of a four-poster bed. So my sexual experience had been limited by curfew and several layers of clothing.

Amanda was another variation on the theme. She pulled the tails of her shirt out of her jeans. "Well? I'm not doing everything. I said you could kiss me." She took a wad of gum out of her mouth and placed it beside her on the sand, a prim and rather delicate gesture. I had an unsettling vision of her putting it back in her mouth when we had finished for the evening.

She had long, straight brown hair and a wide face, sur-prisingly pliable lips and a playful tongue. She wore braces, which was a bit of a danger—one had to be careful or the cuts could be severe and take forever to heal—and I could taste, in addition to the whiskey and the grape gum, onion and garlic and pepperoni. Pizza for dinner, I thought, and no mints for this girl. Her bra was something of a mystery, but she was patient while I struggled, and while my attentions were elsewhere she used the opportunity to suck so hard on my tongue that even a day later it felt as though something had torn.

"So what are you doing at Lamberts'?" she said during a pause in our labors. "Why aren't you at Malibu or Zuma?"

We had been tussling for an hour, and I had discovered certain limits: fondling her small, bare breasts was acceptable, rolling on top of her, my legs between hers, was not; stroking the small of her back made her hum, but when my hand drifted lower, she kneed me, and I was fortunate that her aim was slightly off.

"My parents are in Germany," I said. "They're thinking about getting divorced, and whenever they think about getting divorced they like to take little trips and spend a lot of money."

"Germany's not a little trip."

"No, that's why I think it might be serious this time."

"Mine have been divorced for two years. Mom's living in an ashram, so we stayed with our dad."

"Sorry."

"It's no big deal. They yelled a lot before they split up, so this is better, I think. Not so much crossfire."

Our kissing changed then from the violent imitations of the biting and chewing we had seen on movie screens to something quieter, friendlier.

"There now. This is nice," Amanda said. "Don't you think?"

"Sure." We were pecking away at each other like a couple of birds. It was nice, sure. Delicious, I might have said, to lie next to someone who seemed easy enough to be with. Though

I admit I was also wondering how I might relieve her of her jeans and how I could protect myself in the event of discovery.

Amanda kissed me good morning in front of her father's house just as a gray band along the eastern horizon signaled dawn. She squeezed my hand, and we promised to meet when the others did, knowing that Freddy and Gale, Duncan and Sheila had already made plans for tonight.

"I had a good time, Fish."

"Me too."

She carefully opened the screen door, and I waited until she waved to me from her window upstairs, then I drifted uphill toward the Lambert property. I had not wanted to be here originally; in the days after my parents had announced their plans, the word *abandoned* had taken possession of my thoughts like the tune of a commercial that, by its insidious nature, is impossible to shake. And yet the Lamberts had proven to be much more parental than my own mother and father, Freddy was the older brother I had always wanted but never had, Mira was Mira, and Amanda was a welcome bonus. I was dazed by bourbon, the proximity of sex, and the goodness of my good luck, and I would have been happy to curl up in the bushes bordering the Lamberts' house. Freddy, however, was pacing at the bottom of his driveway. "Come on. We're late. The old man finds out, I'll be cutting firewood every night this summer. And you won't be getting any more Amanda pie."

We entered the house the way we had exited, the sun forming an orange corona behind Mount Hood as we stepped through the window to my room. Freddy headed off to the shower—his father had arranged a job for him with a

construction crew, and work started early each morning—
while I pitched forward onto my bed. Only to discover that I
was wide awake. Again. So far, for the ten nights of my stay
with the Lamberts, I had slept badly if at all. I would walk upstairs yawning my head off, but the moment my head hit the
pillow my brain would begin to churn as if some poltergeist
were forcing me to replay the day's events. With Amanda in
the picture, it wasn't a wholly unwelcome task. *If only I could
get some sleep.* I thrashed around in bed, trying to think of all the
tricks said to cure insomnia, only to play hell bridge with
Mira a few hours later, agreeing to meet her tonight. It would
work out okay, I told myself. I would listen to more of Mira's
nonsense, then there would be Amanda: a reward for the
courtesy. The summer was turning out to be more interesting
and more complicated than I would have thought possible.
And if I got a little rest, I might be able to enjoy it.

Promptly at nine o'clock that evening, Mira knocked on my
door.

"All right, Fish, let's get this show on the road." Clutched
across her chest was the box containing the Ouija board, a
backpack was slung over one shoulder, and like Amanda the
night before, she wore a plaid flannel shirt; given Mira's pre-
occupations, the conjunction startled me as though the two
girls had somehow exchanged bits of body and soul.

"Okay, fine." I stepped into the hallway to go downstairs,
but Mira held up her hand.

"Nope. We go the way you went last night." She pointed
toward my window. "That way."

"Why? We can use the stairs and the front door. Who
cares if we go out now?"

"That way." She was adamant.

"I just followed Freddy. I didn't even look where we were going, I was that scared. We could fall off the roof."

"I trust you."

"I wouldn't," I said. "I don't trust me."

"Chicken."

"You can say that again."

"Chicken, chicken, chicken." And then she started making *buck, buck* chicken noises, which seemed like a pretty cheap trick for a serious theosophist. Shouldn't she have been able to summon the spirit of Claudia Montoya-Jones or whoever to fly her out the window? She was not to be denied, however, and soon enough I stepped out the window. The sun had not yet completely set, so seeing my way was not the problem; my fear of heights, which had not been engaged during the darkness of the night before, was. The slate tiles of the roof threatened to spin under my feet.

"Come on, Fish." Mira pushed me in the back. "Let's go. You've got a date with Amanda Baird at midnight, right? You wouldn't want to miss that."

How she knew that, I couldn't be sure. The likeliest explanation was that earlier this evening she had talked with her brother, but the thought also occurred to me that she had obtained her information from some spirit or other. An idea like that threatened to send me off the edge as literally as her fingers in my back.

"Don't push. I'm doing the best I can."

"Let's go then."

She had things to show me, she said. We managed our way off the roof and down the trellis, then onto a path that led us away from the river. The path climbed a slight rise through a stand of fir and cedar that ended abruptly after less than one hundred yards. The slight incline also fell away with equal abruptness into a smooth slope broken only by the angular shapes of granite monuments, grave markers, and private mausoleums. Some of the older stones sported likenesses of the deceased or the consolation of angels. One of the largest mausoleums, a replica of the Parthenon, suggested that its tenants had progressed to that state of divine wisdom to which we all aspire. As dusk became more profound, the view afforded this city of the dead became more remarkable as well: the dark curve of the river acquired a greater density in the foreground while the lights of the city's east side glittered within its basin made of hills.

"Yes," I said, "it's pretty. No question."

"Maybe so, but it's not what we came here for."

"Oh?"

I followed her down an asphalt walkway that curved around another wall of fir trees into an outlying section of the cemetery, its suburbs if you will. Here the plots were indicated by brass markers, and the grassy field stretched away in uniform barrenness. Only a few pots of plastic flowers provided occasional relief. At the bottom of the hill within a chain-link enclosure stood an aluminum storage shed, and next to that a backhoe was silhouetted in the gathering darkness. Not far from the backhoe were the tarp-draped mounds of dirt from a recently dug hole.

"Here we are," Mira said. She put down the box with her Ouija board, then fished around in her backpack, coming up with a flashlight that she first aimed into the earth, then handed to me. "See anything?"

"No. Should I?"

She shrugged, pulled out a hammer and a rope ladder from the pack, and began to pound two tent stakes into the grass at the lip of the grave, hooking the loops at the top of the ladder around the stakes when she was finished. "Down we go."

"This is stupid," I said. Still, my foot was on the second rung of the ladder. "You really are weird, Mira. You know that?"

She nodded absently. "I don't mind so much." She wedged the flashlight into the wall of soft dirt so its light fanned between us. "Have a seat."

Sitting cross-legged, we faced one another and placed the Ouija board on our knees. Claudia Montoya-Jones had been convinced, Mira said, that the dead were not really dead. They were merely in another dimension where they waited, biding their time before another incarnation. Cemeteries were nothing more than reminders that these two dimensions were no more remote from one another than two rooms connected by a single doorway. One can have a foot in both rooms if one is willing to stand on the threshold. A person of such heightened awareness as Claudia Montoya-Jones could stand on that threshold while she was rinsing out her underwear; Mira felt that as a novice she stood a better chance of success if she were located in the physical actuality of the grave as well as its symbolic sensibility.

"Close your eyes," Mira said. "Be still. This may take a bit."

"Not too long, or I may fall asleep." I yawned with a certain measure of exaggeration. I meant it as a joke, but right then the same trouble that had afflicted my last ten nights took command. What was I doing here? Sitting in a grave with a girl who was, if not certifiably crazy, then at least off center by a goodly margin. The ground on the floor of the grave was relatively soft, yet I seemed to have found the one hard lump to sit on, and try as I might I couldn't find any relief. Did cemeteries have night watchmen? Was our being here some sort of desecration? Certainly it would be a social *faux pas* if not a moral error to be convicted of trespassing in a graveyard. My father, however, would surely find it as amusing as any fraternity prank. He told his own stories of youthful indiscretions. He had once attached a drooping plaster-of-Paris cock to the reproduction of Rodin's *Thinker* that stood watch over the library. He had loads of such stories. But would his own amusement last if he were told he needed to wire money for my bail?

"Spirits, are you here with us?"

Mira's voice broke through my reverie, and I felt the pointer move under my fingers, faster than I could have attributed to my own unconscious desire to be shocked. The pointer slid to the word *YES* and stopped.

"Madame Claudia, please address us, if you can."

The pointer moved away from *YES*, then returned, again with a rapidity I found unsettling.

"Madame Claudia, we have with us tonight a doubter—"

"I never said that."

"—a doubter, who needs to be convinced of the reality of the immortal dimension. He will ask a question that only he knows the answer to. Your answer will be his answer regarding the truth of your existence. Fish?"

"I don't know what to say."

"Ask a question. Madame Claudia is waiting."

"What am I supposed to ask?"

"Anything." She was becoming impatient with me now. "Just ask a question."

"Fine. What's the capital of California?"

"No, no, no," Mira said, "not that kind of question. Everyone knows that. You have to ask something that no one else knows about."

"This is stupid."

"Just do it, Fish."

"All right, let's play your stupid game. What does my father think of Mira's father? There, that's my question."

I expected Mira to move the pointer to a predictable answer, one that would spell out F-R-I-E-N-D, but instead it moved to three letters then stopped.

"S-O-B," Mira spelled, her confusion so obvious that her forehead was creased in concentration. "Sob. What does that mean?"

"Nothing. I told you this was stupid. I've had enough. Look," I said, standing up and upsetting the board and pointer, "this is an idiotic game and you're as nuts as they come."

I climbed the rope ladder as fast as I could, and I thought seriously of throwing it down into the hole, giving Mira a dose of her own symbolic sensibilities, as it were. I could hear her calling to me from the grave, her voice muffled by the damp earth. But instead of waiting for her I began to jog back toward the older part of the cemetery, certain that an evening of exercise with Amanda could make up for the past hour. As I neared the crest of the hill, the markers and monuments again became more elaborate, the sentiments on each stone more roundly effusive of the departed one's value to family and friends. Small landscape lights indicated the turns and intersections of various paths, but in the darkness I lost the landmarks I remembered from an hour before—an angel here, a temple there—and I lost my way. I did not slow down, however, until the dark figure of a man holding a rifle rose up before me.

"Don't shoot," I cried, throwing up my hands. "I didn't mean to be here."

This was the center of the cemetery, and I soon realized that I was pleading with a memorial for a veteran of World War I. Sweat trickled down my neck and back, and as I crouched next to the puttees of this dead soldier of the Great War, I shivered in the cool evening air.

My father maintained that Miles Lambert was "the luckiest son of a bitch on the face of God's green earth." This assessment was probably three-quarters envy and one-quarter admiration since Miles Lambert's material success was in no small part fueled by his marriage and his wife's inherited wealth. And it seemed obvious that the Ouija board was referring to this judgment. "I've done well with what I was given," my father liked to say, "but Miles stumbled into the mother lode, and he still hasn't figured out what he's got."

My father was all too uncomfortably aware that someone his own age, a childhood pal no less, was so much more prosperous than he. It further galled him that Mr. Lambert did not seem to care all that much about the ornaments of affluence but instead preferred to tinker with the old radios that sat on shelves lining the walls of his basement workshop. His wife had a gold mine of old family stocks such as Coca-Cola, IBM, and GM, but Mr. Lambert had had the foresight to diversify into real estate, and my father said he had once owned a quarter of Portland's downtown. And yet Miles Lambert was totally unaffected by prosperity: he drove his antique Buick; his clothes were seldom fancy, jeans and tee shirts the rule; and he derived more satisfaction from a well-played point in squash than the closing of a multimillion-dollar land deal. My father, who was no piker himself when it came to making money, was baffled by such attitudes, since between his own impulses and my mother's, they were usually teetering on the edge of some new precipice of insolvency. Any proof of extra liquidity fascinated my father, who seldom carried enough cash to pay for parking.

I say all this because, although my father would not have acknowledged it, I believe he hoped that the Lamberts' good fortune might rub off on me as well as our family. Maybe the luck that had followed the Lamberts for the last twenty years would follow me home and rescue the Beckers from further fiscal misfortunes. And maybe my exposure to the Lamberts would also put me on a more definite course of maturation.

I was, frankly, a disappointment to my father; he could not resist comparing me to those Christmas-card images of Freddy, who was already over six feet tall and, from acting as his father's squash partner, full of rude animal health. When my father looked at me, he saw what I saw in the mirror every morning: a shapeless, unformed human being, masculine in gender but wholly lacking in what he considered the male gifts—charm and good manners, a distinct understanding of one's vocational calling, and, maybe most importantly, prowess in the recreational activities of the elite such as squash, tennis, and golf. Instead, I had a tendency to wipe my nose with my sleeve, I was a lackadaisical student who did not have a clue—or a care—about my future, and as far as sports were concerned I was as deft as a pile of sand. My hair was too long, his patience too short.

So went my thinking while I sat at the base of that forgotten soldier, under the gun so to speak, all precipitated by Mira's goddamn Ouija board. Madame Claudia had gotten to the heart of things: my father, as much as he loved Miles Lambert out of respect for their shared pasts, thought of him as a son of a bitch, a lucky one. But much worse was the realization of what my father felt about me: I had known it for some time—maybe years—but had never before admitted it to myself with the honesty that, when it strikes, has the force of a cathartic.

Mira found me finally, the beam of her flashlight cutting a swath across the grass, the stones, the legs of the soldier, my face. And then she showed me a shortcut home, another path that ran along the north side of the house, entering the grounds by the swimming pool. Rarely used anymore, the pool, built in the 1920s, had been the scene of many a party. Now, however, the tiles were chipped and stained, the concrete pitted, the water a brackish green. The wrought-iron ladders on either side were art deco–inspired monstrosities, Beardsley women rising from the depths of their murky sea; in the beam of the flashlight the ladders went down into the green water for three inches and disappeared.

"Who's for a swim?" Mira said.

"No thanks, not me. I have a date, remember?"

"With Amanda. How could I forget? Come on, you've got oodles of time."

She snapped the light off, and in two quick movements

she had shucked her shoes and jeans and glasses and plunged into the water, swimming the length of the pool in one breath; when she called again, her voice came from the far end. "Come on in, Fish, the water's fine."

"Not me. I'm going to the house." Through the trees I could see the windows glowing gold, doorways between darknesses. Somewhere down the hill a car started, a radio blared. "Did you hear me, Mira? I'm going."

Silence. A small sound, less than a splash, a ripple maybe. Mira swimming underwater?

"I'm going. Mira?"

Still no response. I felt along the tiles for the flashlight, switched it on, and let the light play along the surface. No Mira.

"Oh, god. Oh, Christ," I said. "Mira." If she were really underwater and in trouble there was no way to see her, no way to know. What would I say to Mr. and Mrs. Lambert when they saw the bloated body of their daughter, green water streaming from her hair, eyes, nose, and mouth? How could I face them if I hadn't tried to help? I was unlacing my shoes when the push came from behind. There are those moments in cartoons when the branch falls, the cliff crumbles, and the character is left suspended in the air, realization of the drop to come just beginning to dawn. I went sailing, and the water took forever in rising to greet me. The air seemed to be a conduit of memory, and the words *so this is how you are born* came to me of their own accord. Then came the water and a darkness ten times more opaque than the night. I swam where I thought a ladder should be, but before Mira could find me with the beam of the flashlight, I went headfirst into one of the Beardsley ladies. Blood ran into my eyes, and the

world, already dark, lost focus as well. I hung on to the ladder with one hand and stanched my wound with the other.
Mira stood over me, dripping, in her panties and the flannel
shirt, the flashlight waving in her hand. As she saw my face
her eyes widened myopically, unaccustomed to vision without the aid of lenses.

"Jeez Louise, you're bleeding."

"You didn't have to push me, you know."

"We've got bandages upstairs."

We trudged up to the house. My clothes were streaming,
my shoes, which I had never had a chance to remove, were
squishy, and I was covered with slime. When I suggested that
we go in the front door like normal folks, Mira nodded her
agreement, and though we wiped our feet we left a trail of
wet footprints behind.

She bandaged my forehead in her room. I lay on the
braided rug while she applied Mercurochrome and gauze.
Her lips were pursed. "I probably ought to get my mother.
You might need stitches."

"It's fine," I said, yawning suddenly, "it's just a cut."

"And you've got a date tonight."

"And I've got a date."

Through her open windows came the intimations of yet
another summer night. Crickets chirruping near the reflecting
pool. The smell of lighter fluid and charcoal burning. The flat
white disk of the moon suddenly swimming into view.

"Did you know," Mira said, "that ten years ago when your
parents came to visit, our fathers had a fight in the gazebo?"

"Who told you that? Claudia Montoya-Jones?"

She looked surprised at the suggestion. "No, my mother
told me. They were drinking Bloody Marys and watching the

sunrise. Our mothers went inside the house to check on the three of us and to scramble some eggs, and by the time they came back outside, our fathers were flailing away at each other. They had just come back from a squash game, so they had their racquets with them in the gazebo. Your father broke a bamboo Slazenger over Daddy's head and drew blood, and that ended the fight, but they never said what started it."

"Probably a let point," I said. "My father hates let points."

Mira had other ideas about the fight, most of which had to do with the souls of our fathers, and when Mira got going on the subject of the soul and theosophical perspectives, there was no stopping her. No doubt Madame Claudia had been busy filling her in on all the juicy tidbits. Their struggle was the struggle of two souls imprisoned too long in corrupted flesh. Our fathers were too concerned with the material rather than the spiritual, and so on and so on.

I didn't make it to the conclusion. Sleep—deeper than any I've ever known, before or since, an enchantment of sleep—at last found me. I remember nothing, not a change of position, not a moment's wakefulness; I may have experienced the impossibility of a night without dreaming. When I woke sunshine was streaming through Mira's opened windows and dust motes twirled in the air like fireflies. Mira was not in the room; her bed had not been slept in. I was alone. I woke with the thought that Amanda would be waiting, that I needed to hurry to the river, that I was only seven or eight hours late. And then I realized just how absurd a notion that was.

Outside, Mr. Lambert was using a long pole with a net on the end to skim leaves and the occasional frog from the reflecting pool. The frogs were frantic in the net, jumping to escape their rescue; upon their release they bounced into the grass, then made for the bushes like a shot.

I stood away from the window and watched from the shadows. I wasn't about to lean on the casement and declare myself. There were too many things I couldn't fathom. Whether my parents loved either me or each other. Why their millionaire friend would do his own yard work, clean his own pool, and look happy in the process. I couldn't imagine my parents and the Lamberts young.

The sky was a deep blue, and the few high clouds could not disguise the mountain or hide the sun; in the reflecting pool was an image of land and sky broken only by the raising and lowering of the dripping, wriggling net and the tracery of an occasional breeze.

3

UN
BEL
DÌ,
1948

In his brief career as a civilian employee of the navy, Miles
Lambert had been stationed on American Samoa as a special-
ist in radar weather forecasting, and although he had felt his
spirit languish in its proximity to military discipline, he often
considered those eighteen months on the island as the best
period of his life. He spent eight hours a day in a radar shack,
hunched over the screens, monitoring the approach of
storms, grading their intensity, and relaying the information
to ships traveling between Honolulu and Sydney. He received reports from other ships and other stations, and by
sharing such information he could compile a fairly complete
picture of what nature was doing in the Pacific. The job was
relatively mindless, there were four sailors rotating the watch
who did the majority of the actual work, and in his off-duty
hours he was left more or less to his own devices.

In the evenings he cruised Pago Pago, a pale, gangly
scarecrow in clothes ill suited for the tropics. He often wan-
dered down by the repair yards; under the glare of arc lights
crews worked around the clock on vessels exhausted by the
recent demands of war and occupation. Other nights he

drifted past the open doorways of the honky-tonks that catered to lonely sailors. The thought that through those doors existed a life altogether different from the life that he himself knew excited and vaguely repelled him. On one such night, when the assignment and the island were both still novel, he saw a native girl with a wilted flower in her black hair delicately slipping a wallet from the back pocket of an unconscious sailor's whites. She saw his curious gaze and, lifting her sarong, displayed quite another flower while her finger invited him. *Come here, big boy.* He shook his head, smiled shyly, and hurried past. During the days he hiked to the top of Matafao Peak and imagined himself one of the first Polynesians, or he lay on the beach and drank Navy Exchange beer, watched the afternoon rain clouds, and, pretending he dictated the moods of sky and sea and cloud, laid bets on the timing of the downpour. He developed a terrific tan.

Home seemed impossibly far away. His mother sent cookies and brownies, his father cut out clippings from the *Herald-Examiner*, and his fiancée, Sylvia, who was impulsive and unpredictable but no letter writer, sewed shirts for tropical climates. The cookies were hardly ever more than crumbles and mold. The clippings were stories of oddities: a calf born with three legs, a man who chopped his mother-in-law into bits with a mattock, that sort of thing. And although Sylvia was a seamstress, the shirts fell apart in the heat and humidity soon after their arrival. A seam splitting, a hem unravelling, a button popping off—these seemed stubbornly indicative of a deeper, darker truth. He longed for a studio picture with a breathy inscription, but he could think of no dignified way to ask. He contented himself instead with a picture of him and Sylvia at his cousin's wedding. He had worn his best suit. She had worn gloves and an orchid corsage. He looked at the snapshot every morning and evening, even though the face in the photograph didn't look very much as he remembered her.

The letters his parents and Sylvia included with their gifts, rarely more than a sentence or two, offered even less consolation: "Hope you're doing well, son." "Bet it gets real hot there, doesn't it?" "Oops, that's all the time I have for now, guess I'll write more later." But they never had more time later and nothing more to say, for they were not, by nature, communicative except through the things they stuffed into an envelope. They would no more analyze an emotion than they would drink from a toilet.

The only letter Sylvia wrote that was more than cursory was the one informing him that she was breaking their engagement and marrying Alan Becker, his best friend from grade school and college. "I am real real sorry," she wrote, "but you never danced enough. We always dance the first two songs, then we sit down and you start talking, and we never get back onto the floor." There must have been a band playing somewhere, he realized, and temptation had grown beyond her strength.

Rather than anger, he experienced a curious relief that he distrusted. He should have been devastated, and he worked hard to acquire the proper attitude, but he couldn't help feeling as though he had been rescued. He had to admit that dancing—all that hopping around—baffled him; he was always counting the time and always getting it wrong. Still, had he been that awful to be around?

The day after he got her letter, he received another, this

time from Alan. "We're unforgivable," he wrote. "You have every right to be sore. I would never in a million years do this to a friend, so I have to believe that Sylvia and I are the result of magic, nothing less. We meet, and it's like drowning. The next thing I know I'm guilty of plotting, deceit, and betrayal. I don't blame you if you never speak to us again, but I'm telling you that no one plans for these things to happen."

Alan and Sylvia had no doubt intended apology and comfort for what they supposed to be his heartbreak, yet he could find nothing within himself beyond a vague irritation. That they could possibly think their actions so devastating seemed ludicrous and sentimental. The sky above Tutuila was blue, the water clear, the palms flapping in the breeze like flags of the isle. Still, he must have experienced some subconscious disturbance of which he was not entirely unaware. His hair—always coarse and sand colored—turned as white and feathery as a cloud over the course of one week; he lost ten pounds, becoming even more gaunt than before. He woke each morning with a clench in his stomach that did not loosen until noon.

Confused by such feelings, which he would never have expected or predicted, he went to several honky-tonks, looking for that head of black hair and that wilted flower, but none of the girls looked familiar; they were all thick waisted and short with the massive arms, legs, and haunches of the tiki gods one saw in the gift shops at Pearl. The last bar he visited, the Happy Conch, was the worst, a putrid, fly-specked disaster where there were no native girls at all, no professionals of any description, and the only patrons were two old men asleep, their heads cradled in their arms on the bar. A rank odor drifted from the pit toilet in the alley forward to the door and out into the street. No one was behind the bar, but

there was a bell of the type found in hotels. He rang it tenta-
tively at first, then more aggressively a second and third time,
until finally a young white woman with short, matted blond
hair emerged from an interior room to greet him. She was
barely five feet tall, a sprite, and he towered above her.

"What?" she yawned, her voice a fog of soft vowel and
indistinct consonant. "You want a drink?"

He hadn't wanted one particularly; he had rung the bell
purely out of exasperation, but now that the woman was here
and because this was, after all, a bar, he asked for a beer.

"With or without a glass?"

He looked around the bar area, at the dirty towels piled
on the floor, the faucet dripping into the sink, the glass with
the cigar butt floating in a half-inch of beer. "The bottle's fine."

"Uh huh."

She did not belong here, he decided, any more than he
did. That much was certain. Wearing a linen skirt and a white
blouse clearly in need of cleaning, spike heels, and nylons—an
outfit that in its better days would have been at home on Madi-
son Avenue—she was no less unexpected than an Eskimo in
mukluks. As she rinsed glasses and emptied ashtrays, she
moved with a frailty that he associated with the elderly and the
palsied. Her heels kept catching in the weave of the mat, and
Miles was prepared to rush behind the bar to help her to her
feet. When she lit a cigarette, the lighter shook in her hand.

The room was still but for the motor of the ancient ceiling fan. It was, Miles felt, an uneasy silence: an odd sensation
to be the only two conscious people in a room, separated by
no more than the three feet of the bar, yet not to talk. "You
don't own this place, do you?" he asked finally for want of
something—anything—to say.

She snorted through the cigarette smoke. "This godfor-saken dump? What do you think I am? Eh, Telofa, who am I?"

One of the old men opened his eyes and said, "You are a goddamn princess-lady."

"You are so, so right." Then, turning back to Miles, she said, "Telofa over there owns the joint. He's keeping me on until my money comes. A few problems at home to straighten out, you know, then I'm on my way again."

"Sure. Problems."

"Meanwhile, I get to sample Telofa's watered-down whiskey." She poured herself a drink in a shot glass, then downed it at once. "It could be worse."

The effects of the drink were immediate: her voice gained clarity, her balance improved. A spot of color spread from below her eyes to her jaw. He had never seen such rapid changes except in time-lapse photography.

"How could it be worse?"

"There might not be a Telofa or a Happy Conch at all." She shrugged, ran one hand through her hair. "Egad, I'm a mess. Eh, Telofa, how you let me get this way?"

The old man smirked into his arms. "I tried to stop her, didn't I?" he said, elbowing his fellow sleeper without any vis-ible response. "I try to stop her," he said to Miles, "but the goddamn princess-lady gets her way, you know?"

He began to frequent the Happy Conch on a daily basis. He never came at a time when Ariana wasn't there because she was never not there. She never seemed particularly pleased to see him, but she wasn't unhappy either, and he took that as encouragement. She seemed willing to be with him mainly because they were the only two non-natives to frequent the

Happy Conch; there were plenty of other sailors and officers on the island, of course, but the Happy Conch was so far down the ladder of social desirability that only Samoans ever darkened the door. In November she ate Thanksgiving dinner with him in the officers' mess; in December they celebrated Christmas and the new year in the hangar that had been converted to a gymnasium. She proved to be as awkward as he on the dance floor, and she seemed genuinely happy to sit down after one or two songs, though her willingness to sit might have had more to do with the difference in their heights than with any wish for conversation. In fact, he had learned remarkably little about her except what he could see with his own eyes. She drank constantly, yet was never quite drunk. She chewed her fingernails to the quick. Her clothes—never quite clean—suggested money, but she never had any that he saw. She gave orders like a general or a duchess, someone accustomed to being obeyed. Then again, she often seemed unmoored—as though, waking from a nap, she no longer knew where she was. She showed little curiosity about his recent past and even less inclination to supply any information about her own. He had supposed that she would be leaving soon, but days came and went, and there was no more mention of problems or home, money or moving on. He wanted to ask her about her family, where she was from, and how and why she had gotten here, but he feared that the mere mention of a life beyond the island might be enough to pull her away.

The commander of the naval station, Captain Williams, noted the new addition on the arm of the civilian weather officer, and he complimented Miles during a pause in the New Year's dance.

"Leave it to a civvie," he said, lighting a cigar, "to find the only single white woman in a thousand miles. You take care, son, they're a rare commodity out here in the islands."

"Yes, sir."

"White girls don't handle the tropical life too well, the single ones at any rate. They come here, running away from their mamas or their boyfriends, thinking they'll go native, wear colorful fabric, put flowers in their hair, that sort of thing, but for most of them it runs counter to their nature, they're too interested in organizing things, and it's hell to organize when all you feel like doing is lying around sipping on drinks with funny names. Married women are another story entirely. If they marry white, they boss us around, get us all heated up, then they organize us. A little touch of home, you know. We're supposed to come up with Christmas trees and snow, however we can get it, and being civilized white men we do what we can until our ears bleed and our dicks rattle in our drawers. Everything gets stowed away shipshape when you're organized. They love to make us earn it.

"But if they come out here and marry native, they'll just get told to rethatch the hut."

It was assumed by all in the navy community that Ariana had been organizing Miles for quite some time. It was, however, not so simple a matter. There was, first and foremost, the problem of privacy, of where they could be together without an audience. In the officers' quarters Miles shared a room with an ensign from Oklahoma. This in itself was not insurmountable; there are rules of decorum in such situations—a tie on the doorknob, a sign in the window—but it so happened that the ensign was also a zealous Baptist, and his condemnation of Miles's intentions was explicit and left no room for misunderstanding or further discussion.

The back storeroom at the Happy Conch was even less suitable. The first time Miles ventured through its curtain, Telofa and the other elderly fisherman began to chant and pound the heels of their hands on the bar. Miles could imagine that such sounds had been produced on the sides of dugout canoes for centuries.

The light was dim, a yellow twenty-five-watt bulb. Like those of the bar itself, the exterior walls were thatch and smelled like compost; the interior wall was a cast-off sheet of wallboard. His eyes were drawn to the meager furnishings. A cot, and next to it an open suitcase holding a pile of underclothing. A wire ran from one side of the room to the other, and hanging from it were two blouses, a skirt, and a hand towel, all damp to the touch. Two oil drums held empty bottles. The walls breathed mold and decay. There was no window. Through the curtain came the hoarse voices of Telofa's patrons, friends who called the Happy Conch a home away from home.

"Nice," he said.

"Don't be an idiot. It's a rat hole."

"So move."

"Where?"

"Wherever. Someplace else. Anywhere but here."

"That's easy enough to say," she said, "but I've made my bed. And if you can't understand that, then leave me be." She stood at attention. "The hell with you."

He recognized the argumentative tone, but what position had he taken? He put his hands on her shoulders to pull her to him, but she shrugged him away.

"No."

"What? What did I do?" He leaned forward to nibble on one of her perfect ears. Tiny, perfect shells, so different from his own, which reminded him of a basset hound's.

"Stop it. I told you. I've changed my mind, this will never work here. Just go."

But a moment later she changed her mind again, offering him a seat on the cot with a pat of one hand. From underneath the underwear in the suitcase she pulled a portable phonograph and with it a single recording. She cranked it carefully, and Puccini's Butterfly was given a voice of quavering hope:

> *Un bel dì, vedremo*
> *Levarsi un fil di fumo sull'estremo*
> *Confin del mare.*
> *E poi la nave appare.*
> *Poi la nave bianca*
> *Entra nel porto, romba il suo saluto.*
> *Vedi? È venuto!*

Butterfly sang of one fine day, of a ship on the horizon, of her dream of her love reappearing, and Ariana, whose back had been as straight as a plumb line, slowly began to crumple. Her chin trembled. "My trim white vessel," she cried, touching the wisps of his white hair. She crawled into his lap, her body wracked by convulsions of sobbing. Telofa and his friends clustered around the curtain to listen while the cot creaked under the weight of the princess-lady and her giant friend, and when the recording was through they stood by the curtain expectantly, waiting for the scratching of the needle to be replaced by the sound of something they better understood.

In January the first of the season's storms moved through the area, and Miles spent a greater number of hours in the radar shack plotting their course. A tropical depression formed west of Tahiti, tornado warnings originated near Tonga, a series of water spouts was observed by spotter planes south of Oahu. Bands of rain clouds slammed into the Samoan islands in daily formations. Pago Pago was awash, and the ships in the harbor pulled at their chains. Green spray filled the radar screens without pause; barometer readings never rose above twenty-eight. A seaman on a destroyer was washed overboard north of Fiji, and a freighter swamped ten nautical miles from the safety of Pago Pago's harbor. One sailor and the cook were the only survivors.

One night in the midst of the storms Miles opened the door to the Happy Conch to find the bar lighted by votive candles. The generator had gone out yet again, there was no radio, the beer was getting warm, and the pit toilet was as dark as a tomb. It didn't really matter, however, as Ariana was the only one there. Not even Telofa had ventured out. Tonight was not *un bel dì*. She sat on a bar stool, chewing her fingernails, her face flickering in and out of the candlelight.

"Just the man I wanted to see," she said when he opened the door. He lifted his hat and slicker away from his head and shoulders, and water poured out onto the floor. "No, no, don't take those off. We're going out."

"Out? In this?"

"Sure. A walk on the beach, a stroll through the woods. What do you say?"

"I'd rather take a dance lesson."

"Oh, but it's lovely. The torrents, the wind, the primal forces of nature."

"No. I've been out, I've seen it, Jesus god, we're on the fringe of a cyclone. I don't want to go out again."

"Don't be a stick."

He pulled on his slicker again, against his better judgment. She was nuts, there was no getting around it. He had been spending time with a crazy woman, and here was the proof. Water coursed down the street; wind tore at the palms with a noise that sounded like static. In the past two months she had displayed little more than a warm reserve, but with the prospect of imminent natural disaster, she was as manic as a jaybird.

"Come on, Ishmael, don't be such a ninny."

In the face of such insults, what could he do? She was already running ahead of him down a narrow, twisting lane of shacks and hovels, her green poncho practically invisible in the darkness. He followed, holding his hat against his head, ducking under the force of the wind. She was running toward a grove of coconut palms bordered by copra sheds. How could she possibly keep her feet in those idiotic shoes? The footing had long since turned to slime, the slick mud forcing him to skate as well as run, and he felt like the proverbial idiot who cannot walk and chew gum at the same time. He slid in the mud more than once, yet even when he was sprawling, he kept the bobbing silhouette of her poncho in view. Until he went down one last time and lost her. Nothing. Not even the ghost impression the hopeful eye creates in the dark. She might as well have run up a tree and hidden among the coconuts. The sound of the rain among the palm fronds was deafening. He stood still, letting the rain wash him clean of the reddish mud.

"Mi-i-i-les." Her voice was weak and indistinct, with none of the exuberance of just a few minutes before. "Oh, Christ. I'm down here, Miles. I seem to be stuck."

It took some minutes of calling back and forth before he found her half buried in mud and debris. The north side of the coconut grove ended just above a five-foot drop, and she had gone barreling over, along with the rain and the runoff, and now she couldn't move. Something was wrong with her ankle too, she thought.

"I slid into something," she said, "or something fell on me. I don't know. For a moment I was back home, walking through the cemeteries. I was there, now I'm here."

He could barely see her even when he stood next to her, and when he tried to help her up, holding her by her armpits, she gave a short yip of pain before slapping at him to stop. Her legs were pinned, and something heavy was lying across her abdomen.

"Let me find a light or something."

He ran back through the grove, vaguely aware of the palms straining in the wind and rain, the fronds snapping off like fingers. He fumbled through two of the copra sheds before he found what he was looking for: matches and a lantern, a shovel and a machete. By the time he returned mud was sliding down the embankment and washing around her shoulders and into her ears. In the glow of the lantern her face was ashen, her eyes darting, blinking away the froth of rain and mud. She had run into a stack of the grove's refuse piled for burning—fronds and palm bark and coconut hulls—and had managed to tip it over on herself. The trunk of an ancient tree had rolled off the pile, knocking the wind out of her for a moment or two before she had been able to call for him.

"Oh, so you came back after all," she said. "Good. This would have to be the most goddamned stupid way to die."

"People," he said between efforts to move the palm trunk, "don't die from a walk in the rain."

"You don't think so?" she said. She had begun to weep from pain and fear. "You ought to meet my mother. She could drown an elephant in a thimble."

If the world is a series of Rube Goldberg relationships, one *non sequitur* colliding with others and creating still more, then in Ariana's mind at least, her mother was directly responsible for her being buried in the mud and trash of a coconut grove. If not for her mother, she wouldn't have fled Oregon for what she had hoped would be the paradise of island life, she wouldn't have been so foolish as to think that a cyclone was meant to be experienced firsthand, and she wouldn't have gone running over a small cliff in nearly total darkness. For Ariana, Cora Exley possessed the force of a witch who dictated her daughter's fortunes by whim, decree, and not-so-subtle manipulation, and even as she rebelled, Ariana could not be sure that she wasn't doing what her mother intended all along.

Miles learned all this much later. Now, however, using the machete and shovel, he hacked and dug Ariana out of the mountain of garbage she had brought down upon herself. The palm trunk proved more stubborn, but it too finally yielded. Her ankle was most definitely broken. Her ribs were sore and hot to the touch. In order to get back to the grove, he had to carry her over his shoulder and scrabble up the muddy incline on all fours, and while she bounced like a sack of rocks on his back, she recited every curse he had ever heard as well as a few Samoan ones new to his vocabulary.

He took her to the base infirmary where the doctor on duty reluctantly examined her injuries. He set and plastered her ankle and wrapped her ribs in elastic bandages. Told her to clean up, get some rest. Morphine tablets for pain as needed. Go easy. Miles stayed with her that night in the back room at the Happy Conch. He swore to love her, but she was already taking off with the morphine, so it didn't really count. Such declarations need a dry run in any event.

In May, with the rainy season over for the year, Miles packed his bags for his return to the mainland. Ariana was going with him; rather, she was taking him to Oregon, to the Exley home, but before they left the island they were married by a navy chaplain in an empty base chapel, their only witnesses the sentry and secretary for the building. Ariana's leg was still in a cast, her ribs were still bandaged, and nothing was healing quite right. As it turned out, she would have to get the ankle reset, her ribs would never feel the same, and when her mother greeted them at the airport she announced that she had planned another wedding for the back patio at the house. They couldn't expect anyone to take a military ceremony seriously, could they? Everything island-fashion would have to be redone.

Shifting his weight from foot to foot, Miles stood in the busy waiting area and watched this first confrontation between his wife and her mother. Ariana, already colorless from fatigue, slumped forward on her crutches. The trip from Pago Pago to Honolulu to San Francisco to Portland had taken two days and three nights, and she was in no condition to mount a defense. Yes, mother, another ceremony would be lovely. Victorious without firing a shot, her mother—stout, gray, imperious—offered her square hand to Miles.

"So this is the magician." She looked him up and down. "My daughter is a free spirit, Mr. Lambert, but then I suppose you've already noticed that."

"I think this can wait, Mother."

"I don't believe it can." Squinting at him as though he were some exotic specimen to be analyzed, she said, "I'm sure she has already told you that I am domineering and tyrannical. She's right in one respect: we do not get along. My daughter has found her own practice of retaliation: she is deliberately rude, headstrong, and defiant. She left, and for three months we didn't receive one word of her whereabouts, her health, or whether she was in any danger. Absolutely not one word. I'm her mother, but she doesn't believe I worry. Then to find out she is at the other end of the earth. Samoa! What was she thinking? I still don't know. She walks the edge of her own slippery slope, and she never has a sense of the dangers she invites. But that's all water under the bridge. If Ariana is happy, I'm happy. And if you're the one to accomplish such a transformation, then I thank you and welcome you to the family."

Platitudes rose in his throat, and he rejected each successive commonplace. How to answer this spiteful old woman? She stood with her fists on her ample hips, her eyes boring holes into his forehead, waiting for some sort of reply.

"You should love your daughter, Mrs. Exley," he stammered finally. "I certainly do."

At this, both mother and daughter uttered the same syllable—"*Hah!*"—as though each thought she had trumped the other.

The contest of wills did not abate with their arrival at the house. Cora showed Miles into a room on the second floor while telling Ariana that her old room on the third floor was just as she had left it.

"We're already married, Mother, remember? Our wedding was two and a half weeks ago."

"We'll make it official in a month, dear. Please humor an old woman. I don't care to invite neighborhood gossip."

"What is she trying to do?" Ariana cried the moment her mother had closed the door. "She's trying to make me crazy all over again. She's trying to set a new record for time: driving Ariana nuts within the first twenty-four hours. I can't take this, Miles, I just can't. She made me crazy when I was a kid, and she'll make me crazy from the grave. What was I thinking?" She grabbed fistfuls of her short hair, slid to the floor next to the bed that had been designated as his and his alone, and began to rock like an autistic.

But in the days before the wedding, Ariana complied with her mother's demands. She slept in the third-floor room, a goddamn princess-lady in her tower, as Ariana put it, with no hair to let down. Miles slept alone in the massive four-poster bed that overwhelmed his room, sleeping poorly, waking often in the belief that he was back in Samoa in the season of storms, his bed a raft in a raging, hostile, and mud-filled sea. His dreams were confused and entangled with the Puccini recording; from late at night until the early hours before dawn Ariana played the portable phonograph, and Butterfly's voice swam through the heavy, liquid air from the open window of her room into his own.

During the day, as a means of frustrating her mother's plans for gown fittings, catering decisions, and decorating schemes, Ariana slept late, often until two in the afternoon. Her mother had already devised the guest list and mailed the invitations, but there was still so much to be done, none of it anything the groom could do. This left Miles free for much of the day, restless and at loose ends. The Exley estate was extensive although, like the family shipyard on Swan Island, in a state of evident decline. The Tudor manor house was a ramshackle warren of nooks and crannies, the terraced gardens losing their shape to unchecked weeds and cracked walls. Quite out of keeping with what he had seen of Ariana's mother; he was surprised that she hadn't martialed her energies against household neglect in the same spirit as she was organizing their second wedding. By the end of the first week he had explored as much as he possibly could—the east gardens, the swimming pool, the pathways through the overgrowth to the river, the cemeteries that bordered three sides of the estate. Just once in that first week, and then only for a brief interlude, did the clouds pull back far enough to reveal Mount Hood glittering like a wet wedge in its corner of sunlight. The sight was breathtaking, yet he had to wonder at the forces of chance that had brought him to this place at this time. Samoa seemed impossibly far, California another lifetime. *What had he gotten into?* That morning he had spoken with his mother and father for the first time since his arrival back on the mainland. Their voices were familiar, of course, but not intimate, as though his memories of his home and childhood had been the result of dreams rather than experience. They wished him well upon his marriage and said they would be coming for Cora's "official" ceremony. His mother mentioned that she had given Alan Becker's name and address to Cora; he and Sylvia might also be attending. She had been flustered when Cora called, and Alan's name had simply popped out. Miles stared at the phone as though trying to gauge his mother's seriousness before he realized that he would be happy enough to see both of them. They had not hurt him before; what damage could they do now? The overcast collected itself, the clouds knitting the fissures of blue together again, lowering themselves like guardians over the mountain, hiding the gods from view.

In defiance of logic and the weather reports, Cora had planned the wedding for the back patio of the house. Ariana and Miles would stand on the flagstones with Pastor Rehnquist and his wife, who would play the organ; the guests would sit in folding chairs on the grass. Miles had raised the issue of the long-range weather forecast, which predicted rain for the week of the wedding, but his future mother-in-law had silenced him with a furious stare of reproach. *How dare he?* Although the climate in the Willamette Valley could be erratic in June, she was convinced that her vision of the event would be contradicted by neither man nor nature; she could bend either to her will. God was another matter, but she chose to believe that He had bigger fish to fry than a Palatine Hill Road wedding.

And on the morning of the wedding, it seemed as if she would have her way. The sun rose behind a clearly silhouetted mountain. The sky grew pink, then brick red, before settling for the white dawn of a clear day. But at noon, with the ceremony scheduled for two o'clock, the clouds circled back into the valley and the air grew thick and gassy with the clear presentiment of rain. Cora paced the patio, willing an alteration of the skies as Miles and Ariana watched.

"Mother, maybe we should bring the chairs in?" Ariana offered.

"No." Her gray eyes snapped onto her daughter's. "No, it'll pass. I'm sure of it."

"At least the organ, then. Mrs. Rehnquist would prefer not to be electrocuted during the Lohengrin, I'm sure."

"Fine." She resumed her pacing as Miles and the minister heaved the organ back through the double doors.

Miles and Ariana watched during the next half hour as mist turned into a drizzle, which became a downpour. Ariana took periodic nips from the flask secreted in the top of her cast. Her mother had nagged her since their arrival to get her leg tended to, but she liked the cast loose and dirty, and its present condition suited her just fine.

"Mother will blow a gasket," she said, "if it doesn't clear off."

"Which it won't," Miles said. He could imagine a radar screen tracking this particular disturbance as nothing but green arcs and green snow.

"Sixty people standing in our living room in wet clothes. They're going to make even this place look mighty small. But she's not going to like the alternative."

"Your mother wanted an outdoor wedding, we'll have an outdoor wedding. And now it's time," he said, kissing her on one cheek, "to go get dressed."

By one-thirty, guests had begun to arrive, and by one-forty-five the dining room, living room, den, and entry had nearly filled with men in suits and women in cocktail-length dresses. They carried umbrellas and overcoats and looked heartily unexcited by the prospect outside; they murmured about contingency plans and watched the rain bouncing off the seats of the folding chairs. The tissue-paper flowers decorating the aisle seat of each row had long since turned to pulp. The organ groaned the opening bars of a Bach prelude, and the sound died in the crowded rooms. The caterers stood among the guests, having no space to set up their tables.

Finally, at ten after two, Cora stood at the top of the staircase and cleared her throat. Mrs. Rehnquist let the last flat fade to nothing. "I'm afraid the wedding will have to come inside," she said in a voice without inflection. "There won't be a great deal of room, but we'll have to make do. When god gives lemons, one must learn to make lemonade."

It was the moment Miles had been waiting for. He and Ariana stepped up behind Cora, each wearing one of the green ponchos they had purchased the day before at the army-navy surplus store on Broadway.

"What Mrs. Exley means," he said, "is that the arrangements will have to be modified slightly. There are enough of these green things for everyone down in the kitchen. You're welcome to 'em. I suggest that you leave your shoes and stockings in the house. It's warm enough, just a little wet. We'll be fine. It'll be an adventure, a little taste of the island life, something to remember the day by."

He had to admit it. Cora was first in line, and she offered no resistance as he helped her maneuver the poncho over her permanent. She refused to take off her shoes, however, and she sat in the first row in her place of honor as mother of the bride, erect and stern, her feet properly shod in sensible shoes. When the ceremony was over she would throw them away.

Miles would have other memories. His mother and father, puzzled but blandly willing—in the face of such absurdity—to go where and do what they were told. His eccentric cousin, Claudia Montoya-Jones, with her green eyes and extravagant gypsy earrings, raising her hands to bless his marriage. Sylvia and Alan, tentative at first but then loudly congratulatory, as though an outdoor ceremony in a squall were the newest innovation. He kissed Sylvia's cheek and shook Alan's hand, glad now that his two best friends of the past had come. They made themselves at home among the Exley friends and relatives. Sitting in their folding chairs, ponchos arranged for maximum coverage, they looked like a field of zucchini.

But most potent of all was the memory of Ariana proceeding up the aisle of grass and mud between the rows of ponchos. Wearing her own poncho, she made her way forward on her crutches, her uncle escorting her one pace to the rear. Miles helped her climb the two steps to the patio, and as they faced one another in front of Pastor Rehnquist, she pulled back her hood. "Made it, by god," she said, blinking the water out of her eyes. "And on a damn fine day. A damn fine day."

4

THE
DEFENESTRATION
OF
DUBČEK'S
HAT

The delay of transatlantic phone calls may have been the reason I didn't immediately understand my father.

"We're going to Prague," my father said for a second time. "Your mother thinks there might be some good buys."

"Prague," I said, "that's Czechoslovakia."

"Good boy. The schools are doing their jobs after all. You behaving yourself? You minding the Lamberts?"

"Yes, sir," I said. My eyes focused only briefly. The mantel clock indicated ten minutes to two in the morning, then faded to a chocolate blur.

"We need to bring you over here sometime. Take you on a tour of Bavaria. See the sights—the Alps, Nymphenburg Castle, the Pinakothek, all that stuff. When the Olympics are here, maybe."

"Sure."

"Your mother sends her love. She'd come to the phone, but she's haggling over a set of beer steins in the gift shop. We'll call when we get back to the hotel here. A week, ten days."

"Okay."

"*Auf Wiedersehen*, Fish."

"Bye, Dad."

The connection was broken, followed by a rush of whistling, an electrical wind. I placed the receiver carefully in its cradle. The silence of the house was broken only by the ticking of various clocks. The Lamberts' ground-floor study, although recently remodeled with new glass-fronted bookcases and refinished hardwood floors, was a mess. Books were everywhere, stacked on the floor, in chairs, on end tables, under lamps. So many books had been crammed sideways onto other books shelved vertically that the glass doors no longer closed. The phone tilted precariously on a stack of paperbacks and magazines. The Lamberts were voracious and eclectic readers, but they were not terribly concerned about housekeeping or organization, a distinct difference from my own house, where nothing was ever out of place and where I had never yet found a thing that was interesting. In the Lamberts' bathroom you might unearth a leather-bound copy of Newton's *Principia* from underneath a coverless issue of *National Geographic*. I had made my own discoveries of a more predictable nature. *Tropic of Cancer*. *Lady Chatterly's Lover*. Freddy had mentioned that Molly Bloom was a hot item in *Ulysses*, but I never could find what he was talking about.

"How are your parents, Fish?" Mrs. Lambert stood in the doorway. She had answered the phone and then shaken me awake to speak with my parents, and now she was wearing a silk robe and slippers. Her eyes were underlined by shadows of fatigue. "Everything okay? It's so late."

My father probably thought he was calling during our dinner hour. The time zones baffled him for some reason; he could never remember if one was supposed to add or subtract eight hours.

"They're fine," I said. "They're going to Czechoslovakia. My mother has her eye on some things."

"Just so long as they have enough sense to stay away from the trouble spots. And enough money to get home." She pulled down *Martin Chuzzlewit*. "Not that we wouldn't love to keep you here beyond the summer. Freddy and Mira enjoy having you around. As do Miles and I." She tapped the book in her hand. "If this doesn't put me to sleep, nothing will."

She was an insomniac and a drinker, legendary among the members of her own family for doing the oddest jobs at the oddest times. You might wake up at three in the morning, decide to get a drink of water, and then through a window see this tiny woman in a nightgown, a flashlight and shears in either hand, pruning the roses.

"Thanks for getting me, Mrs. Lambert. I bet you'll sleep tonight."

"Well, I'm not getting my hopes up. Goodnight, Fish. Get some rest."

I tossed and turned for a couple of hours following the phone call. My parents' foundering marriage had been the original impetus behind the trip, but now it seemed as though they were returning to their usual pattern: purchasing everything they could lay their hands on to salve whatever hurts they had inflicted upon one another. I replayed each moment, the nuance of each sentence, but the one question that I most wanted to ask was always silent, and the answer was always missing. *Can you love each other?* Try as I might, I could not force a response, no matter how imaginary. In fact, the more I thought about my parents, the less real they became. Eight thousand miles away, they existed only in rare phone calls that contained little more news than a haiku. Their letters were few, postcards more typical, and those held so little white space one could not write much more than an address. I already had quite a collection from their various jaunts around the country: the Bavarian Alps, the Bundestag, the Black Forest, the Autobahn, the Heidelberg Tun, and the Cologne cathedral, among others. There was a globe in my room, and in moments alone I often found myself tracing the distance between Oregon and Europe as though my fingers could somehow find the connection my imagination had denied me. Germany became more concrete even as I lost faith in my parents' existence apart from me. I felt myself growing older at a significantly faster rate, while my parents remained the age they were when I last saw them; the longer they stayed away, the closer in age we became. By the end of the summer we would no doubt be trading off-color jokes and stock tips and recipes as if we were old chums; or worse, I might be expected to shelter them from the storms of their own making.

My father had been right about one thing, however: I lost myself at the Lamberts'. Their house was an island unto itself, and it was possible to believe that no other world existed. I had never known individuals more intellectually curious or more politically oblivious. This was 1968, and in the past six months I had sat through two school assemblies in which our principal announced that yet another American leader had been assassinated. The world was falling apart, but the Lamberts read the *Oregonian* for book and theater reviews; the front page they left alone. Listening to Mr. and Mrs. Lambert talk, one would have thought that the most important debate involved the schism between Freud and Jung in 1914. Or Mira might have you convinced that Madame Blavatsky, Annie Besant, and Jakob Boehme were names you needed to know. Other, more current events—such as Vietnam or marches for civil rights—did not seem to register with the same impact.

I had never known such a place! The house was one nook and cranny after another; hidden staircases and closed-off rooms demanded exploration. The library with its stacks of books invited another sort of investigation. The grounds surrounding the house and the gardens were extensive and thickly forested. Paths led through the cemeteries to the river. At the lowest edge of the property was a family plot where Mrs. Lambert's grandparents and parents had markers. There was also a stone for Mr. and Mrs. Lambert with their birthdates already inscribed. I could have hiked the hillsides for a week and never taken the same pathway twice.

On the weekends and in the evenings Freddy and I played round-robin squash with his father. There was a ramshackle court on the downhill side of the pool. The paint on the front wall was chipped, the boards of the floor were warped where the roof had leaked, and knowing the court gave Freddy and Mr. Lambert a great advantage. I was not in their league, though, not even close. Mr. Lambert gave me two old racquets and encouraged me to work on my game so that when my parents returned I could give my father a lesson. He gave me some pointers about my forehand and backhand. I practiced every afternoon, and as the summer wore on even I could tell there had been some improvement.

Mr. Lambert, who knew my parents better than anyone, seemed to understand what the summer meant to me. Many evenings I sat with him in his basement workshop while he worked on his collection of box radios, testing vacuum tubes and rewinding tuner coils. He told me some of the same stories I had heard my father tell about Miss Florio, and I could pretend I was home. He seemed genuinely glad of my company as well, for some vague tension between Freddy and his father smoldered at all times. A question about sandwich meat could turn into an argument; a discussion of Freddy's driving could become a war. Freddy's job with the construction crew, I learned, was the result of a speeding ticket the previous March; the three cords of stacked firewood were punishment for Freddy's last violation of his curfew. Their squash matches were no longer healthy exercise but battles for control.

It put me in a curious position, watching those two. With his father Freddy could be impossible—irritable, easily offended, truculent. Even a fourteen-year-old could see that. And yet as much as I respected Mr. Lambert, I still followed Freddy out my window every midnight. Amanda Baird had forgiven me for standing her up, but she wasn't about to let it happen again. And while we often were together during daylight hours, it seemed more likely that in the hours after midnight she would finally yield herself to me.

Shadows passed in front of our eyes as clouds played tag with the afternoon sun. Amanda blinked, then sat up on her towel, a frown pulling at the corners of her mouth.

"This stinks."

"What?"

"I'm not getting any sun. Half the time I'm shivering, and the water's too cold to look at."

In front of us the Willamette slid by so smoothly it seemed not to be moving at all. The river was not that far removed from the snow it had come from. And though the day had started warm, every time a cloud caused a shadow the air cooled with a chill more reminiscent of early March than mid-July.

"You have any change?" I asked. "We could take the bus downtown, walk around for a while."

"No."

"No change, or no you don't want to?"

"No."

"Fine. It was just an idea." I rolled over, buried my head in my arms. Amanda was a good scout most of the time, but every now and again she could act as though our being together were not just a summer's convenience.

"What I want to do," she said, "is swim in the Lamberts' pool."

"Jesus, why? It's a mess, trust me. The water's so green there could be shopping carts and snakes and banana peels from ten years ago. A whole Peterbilt. Atlantis. You'd never know. I wouldn't swim there if you paid me. Mira's the only one who can stand it, and you know Mira."

When Mira had pushed me in, the water had been cold and opaque and unlike liquid; it seemed more like some sort of primordial ooze—slippery, thick. While I was underwater, I had imagined all sorts of terrors. Horrible fish mutations. Dead cats. I imagined not coming up.

"I wouldn't swim there if you paid me," I said again.

"I don't care. I don't care how dirty or old it is, I just want to swim in a backyard pool that doesn't have plastic sides."

"You'll care when you see it."

"I won't." She had already begun to gather her towel, the radio, and her Harlequin, throwing them into a tote bag with brisk movements that spoke anger and resentment. "I won't care at all. If it's that gross, I'll look at it and think about what it might have been."

I followed her up the hill and through the cemetery that bordered the east side of the Lamberts' property, hoping there would be no interments in progress. Officially, the roadways through the cemetery were private, and the cemetery security guards were known to give pedestrians a tough time, especially kids in bathing suits and towels. It was all a mourner needed during those final moments of consigning a loved one to the earth—to see some punk in baggies or a bikini come strolling through the ceremony. It gave the cemetery a reputation for being less than respectful. Walking the extra half-mile around the cemetery, at least during daylight hours, was the safer course; night was another story and didn't matter so much.

I mentioned this to Amanda, suggesting we take one of the newer paths that circled the main sections of the cemetery, but she either didn't hear me or chose not to. She marched forward in the middle of the main roadway, heading straight into the path of an oncoming cortege, stepping off to one side only when it became absolutely necessary. I could see the hearse driver's jaw muscles clench.

I grabbed her by the arm. "Easy," I said, "we don't want to get arrested or something."

"Why not?" she said. "What else have we got to do?"

We were not arrested, but because the driver had a radio and had used it, we endured a stern, finger-waving lecture by the

fat security guard at the main gate. Private property. Respect
for the living as well as the dead. Trespassing. Misdemeanor
punishable by a fine of . . . Observation of the proprieties.
How would you feel if . . . ? The guard was so fat his gunbelt
cut him into two swollen pillows, his finger a sausage waving
in the air in front of our faces. We were lucky he didn't call
the Portland cops. Amanda pulled her beach robe together
and stared at the ground, so I was left to nod and make agree-
able, repentant sounds. We were sorry, we'd never do it again.
Yes, sir. No, sir. We walked the rest of the way to the Lamberts' in silence, and only when we had stepped through the
gate and stood next to the pool did Amanda say anything to
me. "I should have pulled down my top, given that fat asshole
something to shout about." Then, "You're right," she said.
"The pool's pretty gross." She pulled off her sandals, sat down
on the coping, and let her legs dangle, her feet no longer vis-
ible in the murk. "Still, it must have been nice once. How
could they let it get this way?"

"They've been remodeling the house, and they can only
work on one thing at a time," I said. "They're planning to fix
it eventually."

"Why wait? They're rich as sin. Well, whoever cleans up
this shit will have a lousy job. No joke." She stared at the
green water for another moment, sighed, then stood up. She
stretched out her towel next to the edge. "At least it's finally
warming up."

She lay down on her stomach and unhooked the strap of
her halter. The quiet was remarkable. Sheltered in a shallow
depression below the house, the pool was insulated from
whatever traffic noise might filter up from the highway, the
only sound that of two honeybees who, in a complicated *pas*

de deux, leaped across the surface of the water, touched down, and then were off again. Above us was the back of the house, the dark windows of the bedrooms overlooking our every move. A curtain curled from Mira's room on the third floor and snapped each time the fickle breeze caught it. The globe that sat on the window bench in my room showed up dark and bulbous from below. We were alone. Mr. Lambert was downtown, Mrs. Lambert was in Lake Oswego at her analyst's, Freddy was at work, and I had not seen Mira since breakfast. Amanda had fallen asleep. Her smooth brown back, bisected by the faint line of the now displaced strap, rose and fell in a steady machinery-like rhythm. The pale swell of one breast threatened to expose itself as she shifted in sleep. I envied Amanda her ease. Her parents had been divorced for two years, her mother was living in an ashram in southern Oregon under the guidance of a swami who owned a fleet of Rolls Royces, and she and her sister lived with their father, a letter carrier who had become distracted with the chronic anger of the abandoned. She had found a way to say "I don't care" with a sound that was nearly genuine, and I knew there were certain things she could help me discover beyond the curve of her hip or the taste of her tongue after she had smoked one of her father's Marlboros. I also knew that living at the bottom of the hill from the Lamberts', she had never imagined that their swimming pool could be stagnant, filled with pondwater and exuding the smell of algae and scum.

I lay down next to her, timing my breathing with hers, and managed to fall asleep, only to have some kind of crazy dream, something about jumping from my bedroom into the green water of the pool, an impossibly far distance. In my dream Mira and Mrs. Lambert claimed that it could be done by those who looked deeply enough into themselves. Encouraged by their confidence, I dove, only to land with a thud on the back lawn, parts of myself strewn about the thick green grass. But like that witless coyote of the cartoons, I managed to reassemble myself, go back upstairs, and try again, time after time. Occasionally Freddy and Mr. Lambert would give the pep talk; they would speak about vectors and wind velocity and lift, but the result was always the same.

I woke, sweating and breathless, on a thud so violent the world seemed to crack. The sky was clear, the sun hot and hazy, though there was another bank of clouds forming in the northwest. Amanda slept on, the line from her strap turning pink. The water looked more inviting than it had half an hour earlier. I stepped in at the shallow end, watching my body disappear. It wasn't so bad. Almost comfortable. The water rose above my waist, shoulders, and head as I followed the slope of the bottom. I took a deep breath, and when my eyes ducked below the surface, I suddenly became sightless, like one of those creatures that lives so deep in the Marianas Trench that there is no light, its eyes no more than vestigial organs. At the far end, Amanda still lay stretched out on her towel. Two gentle frog kicks and I was next to her, just below the coping blocks. It was nothing to slap a little of that green water and let it splash down on her back, and it was easy to duck below the surface, holding my breath. And it was a cinch to grab her shoulders when I came back up and pull her into the water with me. She screamed, but she came up laughing so hard she gave herself hiccups: "You are a *hic* sack of *hic* shit." Her top had fallen off when I pulled her into the water, and we found it only when we thought to look in one of the defunct skimmers.

That afternoon we played like otters in the green water, disappearing from one another in a choreography of surprise attacks and escapes and hysterical embraces. Then finally back to the towels, which the breeze in our absence had carried down the hill. We lay in the last of the sun, our fingers interlaced, our eyes closed to the clouds filling in the empty sky above us. For an instant I was able to believe that this moment was fixed, time at an impasse: the summer would proceed without threat or interruption, and my parents' marriage, although distant, would always be secure.

But the shadow of the house eventually reached us, and Amanda said, "I guess we've had as much fun as we're going to have. I better get home, anyway. It's my night to make dinner."

"More mac and cheese?"

"What else?"

They had cases of the stuff. Ever since their mother left, she and her sister had been living on boxed noodles because their father would eat nothing else—breakfast, lunch, or dinner. Their dinner was conducted in silence so their father could read literature from their mother's swami. He didn't understand it, nor was he interested, but Amanda and Sheila gave the old man credit for trying to see his ex-wife's point of view.

We got up reluctantly, folded our towels, and traded kisses. Amanda refused my offer to walk her home; she needed the time, she said, to get reacclimated to the real world. The walk downhill was a social and economic descent, and she didn't need any distractions.

Before she could begin the walk home, however, there was one last discovery: the globe from the window of my room, resting in the rosebushes. How did it get here? I wondered. Looking up at the window, I could have sworn I saw shadows.

"The wind?" Amanda said without much conviction.

"Maybe," I said. "I guess so."

Spinning the world on its axis, my fingers found Germany by instinct, then crept to the green blot that was Czechoslovakia and the dot that was Prague.

"This," I said, offering the globe to Amanda, "is where my parents are."

My father began the following letter on a postcard of Hradčany Castle. He had much more to say, however, than could be contained on one postcard, so his message was continued on cards of the Holy Child of Prague, Waldstein Palace, and the Old Synagogue, all of which were enclosed in an envelope and mailed from Heidelberg.

Dear Fish,

You've no doubt read about the excitement brewing in Czechoslovakia. The entire political situation is undergoing a kind of reformation, controls of one sort or another being loosened. The leader of this revolution, a very self-effacing Slovak named Dubček, has taken on the status of rock star, even in ironic Prague. He is bigger than the Beatles or Elvis, I dare say. Kafka must be doing backflips. Needless to say, your mother and I knew less than nothing about it when we arrived. Your mother was only interested in obtaining a silver tea service, even though I told her she was more likely to come home with a Skoda tractor or several cases of Pilsen beer.

Our first night in Prague, we had no more settled into our room at the Hotel Splendid when there was a rather officious knock at our door. Since

*this was our first foray into a Communist country, you might well imag-
ine our apprehension. Papers, papers, papers! Where were our
papers—passports and so on. At the door were three men in dark suits.
Your mother says that the tailoring and the cloth were not bad, not what
one might expect after reading the* Herald-Examiner *where Warsaw
Pact countries are described as Polish jokes with advanced military hard-
ware. The men had wrestlers' necks, but they spoke a polite, though stilted,
English. First Secretary Dubček wished to speak with us. Oh, he did, I
said. And what would the First Secretary want with two vacationing
American tourists? First Secretary Dubček would have to explain, they
said. So we sat down to wait for the good Mr. Dubček and the five of us
waited for five or ten minutes, and then I thought, these boys look okay, so
I offered them a shot of bourbon from the flask we keep under your mother's
lingerie. The one named Ludvik shook his head, sending the other two outside, and I thought I had unknowingly breached some law of Communist
propriety, but soon enough they returned with a bag full of Pilsen and two
bottles of unlabeled schnapps. The First Secretary might be a while in coming? I said. He is a very busy man, they said, nodding, and there is a great
deal of pressing business clamoring for his attention. But don't worry, he
will be along as soon as he possibly can. In the meantime . . . Well, we at-
tacked the schnapps and beer, and Ludvik, Karel, and Josef were very
convivial drinkers, although I don't think they had more than a glass or
two of the beer and nothing of the schnapps. But very friendly. They urged
us to enjoy ourselves in their country.*

*By the time First Secretary Dubček arrived, your mother and I were
not very well suited to polite discourse, I'm afraid. Karel had brought a radio
along with the hootch, and your mother and I were dancing to some balalaika music when Mr. Dubček announced himself at our door. "Oh," he
said, Ludvik interpreting, "the music of our Soviet brethren. Our comrades,"
he grimaced. By this time, there was no stopping your mother, you know
what dancing is for her. It so happened that Mr. Dubček was wearing some*

sort of ancient straw boater. The day was warm, the sun bright, but that hat was an absolute riddle! I have no idea how he might have come by it or why he would be wearing it, not a correct piece of socialist attire whatsoever. It could have been a prop in a museum piece—Calvin Coolidge comes to Prague. Your mother took one look at that piece of 1920s haberdashery and burst out laughing, pulled it off the First Secretary's head, and sailed it out the window, which had been opened for the pleasure of the summer breeze off the Vltava. It flew for a great distance and skipped along the cobblestones. You can imagine—the party stopped on a dime. Until Mr. Dubček himself started to laugh. "The Defenestration of Dubček," he said again and again. His aides began to laugh uproariously. Some sort of historical allusion, I learned. "We shall be lucky indeed if I don't go flying along with my hat," he said. "And maybe you'll fly with me, too," he said, pointing to his aides. He has a remarkable sense of humor for such a potato face, but I'm not sure that Ludvik, Karel, and Josef enjoyed the joke as much as he did.

Our visit got to cases pretty quickly after that. He is in a tight spot; the Russkies are making his life a high-wire act with fire instead of a net. Since January he has lifted censorship, moved toward democratization, but the country is in desperate need of economic reform. The Soviets are threatening an embargo. Mr. Dubček is looking for any source of capital, even from the West, although that is hush-hush, given Brezhnev's tendency to frown like a dead man. He knew I was an investment banker. Was I looking for potential partnerships with a progressive socialist state? Was I able to steer anything his country's way? "The democracies of the West have yet to redeem themselves for 1938," he said. He held my hand much longer than men do at home, his eyes searching for something. I tell you, Fish, I felt pretty small telling him I wasn't that big a cheese: I was in his country on purely personal reasons, I didn't have my finger on the kind of capital that would help him, and I had no official clearances or authorizations. I couldn't help him unless he wanted to underwrite a shopping mall in Torrance.

He got out of there pretty quick once he saw how small an operator he had collared. He and Ludvik, Karel, and Josef marched out of the Splendid and up Ovanecka like thieves on the lam, which, given the desperate nature of their situation, was pretty much the case. I felt bad not to help the guy. He's a straight arrow, and the walls are closing in on him. But in Prague, the moment is everything—they would make spring the only season of the year. Your mother and I watched Dubček head toward the castle. He saw what was left of that hat of his. He picked it up and sailed it, a regular Frisbee toss, an exceptional heave, and though they were too far away for us to hear, I could see that he and his boys were having themselves a fine laugh at his own expense. An admirable man.

I told Amanda about my father's letter two days after I received it. The Lamberts had been uniform in their appreciation of my father's recording of the event; they were not current with the situation in Prague, but they knew how to look it up, and they soon understood the portent of Dubček's advances toward two American tourists. They each had very different interpretations of what the event signified, however.

"It must be getting desperate, indeed," Mrs. Lambert said, "if your father is perceived as a possible deep pockets."

"That Sylvia, I can just see her dancing to a balalaika," Mr. Lambert said, "and then throwing the First Secretary's hat out the window." Mr. Lambert had had his own experience with my mother's whimsical behavior, and the letter seemed to remind him of other events.

Freddy pulled out that day's paper, in which the Communist Parties of five Warsaw Pact countries appealed to their brethren in Czechoslovakia to "guard with their lives the Leninist principle of democratic centralism."

"It's a warning shot across Dubček's bow, all right," Mr.

Lambert said. He looked at the World News section with an expression that was at once curious and impassive.

"Your parents were in the middle of history," Freddy said, "and all they had was their American Express card."

"No," Mira said, "they threw history out the window. Who knows what resonances were contained in that hat? For Mr. Dubček, for Czechoslovakia."

"They were living in the moment, in eternal spring," Mrs. Lambert said, "and more power to them."

"They were living out a case of mistaken identity," Mr. Lambert mused, "and after an introduction like that, I can only wonder whether they ever got their tea service. Thank god they're back in Germany; when the storm breaks, it's going to be fierce."

Dismissive of the Lamberts since our afternoon by their pool, Amanda offered another opinion entirely: "Your father sounds depressed. Trust me, I know about depressed fathers." We were on the sand by the river. Her sister and Duncan Rhodes were rutting somewhere in the bushes, close enough that we could hear the play-by-play. Freddy and Gale Lewis had disappeared almost immediately after our arrival, and I didn't expect to see him again until he stepped through my window the next morning.

"What does he have to be depressed about? He's in Europe spending all kinds of money and pretending he's the center of attention."

"Let me see the letter," she said, pulling a flashlight from her tote. "Look, I don't think you get it at all. The one time he has a chance to be a mover and shaker he has to admit he's nothing more than a suit in a branch office. Your mother made an impact, but that may have made it all the worse."

"They were drunk and she made a fool of herself, you mean."

"Not likely. It's probably the best moment either one of them has ever had. When my mother left, she climbed into the back seat of the swami's Rolls, and you can bet the swami was waiting there to greet her personally. Two days later my father came home from work, stripped down to his boxers, and started shouting about his potbelly, bald head, and the idiots he had to work with every day. For the next week he brought home all the mail from his route and burned it in the fireplace. He said it was the most satisfying thing he'd ever done, watching all those checks and bills, junk mail and love letters, going up in smoke. He was the most important person in those people's lives, even though they never knew it. He's never done it again, as far as I can tell, but who knows? It beats reading the swami's recipe for brown rice."

I'm not proud of what I did then: I grabbed the letter out of her hand and knocked the flashlight into the sand, muttering something about my father not being the damn mailman. I had been stupid to tell her anything. The Lamberts, I said, had a better appreciation for what what my parents had been through than she did.

"Somebody needs to get a life," she said coolly, noting further, "You ought to know it better than anyone—the Lamberts are just temporary, no matter how you look at it."

I was acting like a four-year-old, and I knew it. But, as the proverb tells us, there is no reasoning with a fool; instead of correcting a mistake he makes another, thinking to cancel his original error by compounding it. I left our spot by the riverside and ran across the highway, angling toward the path through the cemetery, pleased with myself for making so definitive an exit. And angry for being such an ass. Wondering already if Amanda would listen to my apologies tomorrow. Stupid, stupid, stupid!

My childhood was not awful; I had faced no abuse either real or imagined, so I had never considered adults a threat, but I had also discarded any notions of infallibility where my parents were concerned. They loved me, I knew, as well as they were able, but it was a love that could not always overcome their own impediments; I never knew where or in what context the next flaw in the rather thin veneer of their characters might be revealed. Knowing that, I shouldn't have been surprised at Amanda's comparison of our parents, yet I refused to believe that my father might be suffering from some dark night of the soul, an awful uncertainty regarding the value of his life. For to believe that was to deny my father and my mother the superficiality that had been the bedrock of their lives as well as their marriage—their love of material things and their use of credit as a Band-Aid for the psyche. A greater threat to our stability as a family.

The dark shapes of the cemetery at night no longer bothered me; my imagination no longer turned stone angels into griffins, nor did the mausoleums any longer appear as havens of ghosts and demons. The turns and landmarks were second nature, but I could see no use in tempting fate or superstition, no matter how irrational or archaic; I hurried. So I was not prepared when, crossing the back lawn of Lamberts', a zone I considered safe, I was nearly crowned by the globe from my room. It hurtled past my ear before bouncing into the rosebushes for the second time in a week.

The lamp on the end table next to my bed had been turned on, and clearly outlined in the window was Mira. As she turned her head the light bounced off her glasses like sparks.

"You," I said. "Mira." I spoke softly, not wanting to wake her parents, but I knew my voice carried to the window in the still night air. "What the hell are you thinking? You could have killed me."

"Don't be such a ninny."

I picked up the globe, then ran to the trellis before she could bean me with anything else. She was waiting at the window, blocking my entrance.

"I thought theosophists were against violence."

"Sure. That's why I didn't hit you. And how is our Miss Amanda?"

"Let me in, Mira."

"Nobody's stopping you."

I stepped across the casement, aware that in doing so I was trading one world for another. The act seemed irrevocable. Amanda was now on the other side of the window, and Mira looked me in the eye.

When I had first arrived at the Lamberts', I had taken one look at Mira and felt a hole in my stomach, but Freddy had warned me away. She had already convinced me that she was in touch with things better left unknown; I had no desire to lift the lid on that particular box. But as I stepped through the window, I took the hand she offered, and when she looked at me she did so with kindness as well as her usual scrutiny.

"Your parents are in trouble," she said.

"No fooling," I said. "That's why they're in Europe and I'm here."

"I'm not talking about the obvious stuff. I mean real trouble."

"Divorce isn't enough?"

"It's just an hors d'oeuvre before the entrée."

"Cheery news. I take it you've been conversing with your friend Claudia again."

She nodded, biting her bottom lip. "I know what you think. But it doesn't matter. Claudia Montoya-Jones told me that your parents are following a path already decreed by history. When your mother threw the First Secretary's hat out the window, she was replicating forces that had wreaked havoc on a continent. A moment of joy that ends in despair. Their own personal hell is just now beginning. I'm sorry."

She looked sorry for me. Possibly she was sorry for my parents and the unspecified trials she was certain they were soon to endure. Whatever the source and object of her sympathy, it was the same girl who had thrown a globe in my direction not once, I realized now with a start, but twice.

"Goddamn, Mira," I said, "who put the bee up your butt?"

In the morning I went back to the study. The Lamberts had encyclopedias galore because Mr. Lambert made it a habit to buy any set he saw moldering on someone's shelf or lying in the sun at some yard sale. None of their sets was complete and none newer than 1952, but Europe was an old continent and Czechoslovakia an old country, I figured, and I could learn enough. Absorbed with my own concerns—foremost among them the state of my parents' marriage and my own sense of self should that marriage dissolve—I hadn't given much thought to where they were going or how history might prove their undoing; they were simply going from one foreign country thousands of miles away to another. I sat down with volume 4, Christian Science to Dante. Czechoslovakia. I found what I was looking for soon enough.

In 1618, the Hungarian emperor Matthias ignored the *Majestätsbrief* that had granted freedom of religion to those of the Bohemian Brethren and Lutheran faiths. Angry at the deception, members of the Bohemian Diet declared the emperor deposed, and two imperial councillors were thrown from the windows of Hradčany Castle. Strangely enough, the councillors were unharmed by their brief flight, but the Defenestration of Prague, as it was soon called, was the first spark of the Thirty Years War, a conflict that ultimately embroiled much of Europe. Bohemia proclaimed its autonomy, and Frederick, the elector palatine, was elected king. But in 1620 at Bílá Hora, or White Mountain, the Bohemian Protestants were routed by the forces of the empire and of the Catholic League led by Tilly. The battle signaled the end of independence for Bohemia and Prague for three hundred years, Bohemia was ravaged, and those who would be known as Czechs were reduced to misery and servitude. And Frederick, who had expected aid from his father-in-law, James I of England, would forever after be called the Winter King for the brevity of his rule.

5

A TRAIN HEADING SOUTH, 1954

In October of 1954, eight months pregnant with her second child, Ariana Lambert boarded a train heading south. A porter helped her up the steps and into a seat: a tiny woman with short blond hair, her belly preceding her, as stately as an ocean liner gliding into harbor. Her husband, Miles, tall and stooped, his white hair like a beacon, stood where she could see him holding Freddy, their two-year-old, who had obviously begun to cry. Freddy burrowed his head into Miles's shoulder and refused to wave to Mommy. In spite of her resolve not to cry, Ariana felt her eyes fill with water, and one more entry was added to the list of crimes her mother had committed. The platform emptied, the porters pulled their steps inside, and the train began to roll. Miles walked alongside, then jogged as he waved, but soon, too soon, he no longer kept up, and with one final wave he gave up altogether. *I am not doing this,* she thought. *Why am I doing this?* Miles and Freddy dwindled to specks in the dreamy light of dusk, and Ariana fought the wave of loneliness that threatened to swamp her where she sat; then she felt the heavy movement deep in her guts, an elbow or knee pressing against her bladder, reminding her as a point of order that she could not claim to be alone.

Pulling a tissue from her purse, she took stock of her situation. The car in which she sat was nearly empty. It was only a few weeks past Labor Day, and there were no enthusiastic travelers anxious either to start their vacations or to bring them to a weary close. There was neither boisterous laughter, children running up and down the aisle, nor couples surrounded by luggage spilling away from their seats. The train rolled smoothly on tracks paralleling the river, and Ariana could almost believe that it ran through a late afternoon drizzle for her mother's benefit alone, and her gray coffin six cars to the rear.

A stout conductor in a blue uniform pressed through the doors to punch the tickets of the few passengers in the car. He had a meaty, wine-colored face and bushy eyebrows; cigar ash littered his jacket; and he winked at the women who were traveling alone.

"Here we go," he sang, "tickets, please, everyone. Thank you, sweetheart," he said to the grandmother wearing a pill-box hat covered in net and wooden cherries. "And a very nice chapeau that is."

The old lady tittered, and he next waggled those eyebrows at a plump, henna-haired woman who was escorting three teenaged girls to a home economics competition in Eugene. The woman, whose voice had all the delicacy of an anvil, announced her star pupils and their chances for victory, to the acute embarrassment of the girls, who shrieked and hid their bad complexions in their hands.

"Well, I'm sure you'll all be making happy men of your husbands," the conductor said, "sometime very, very soon."

Again the giggles, the eyebrows used as props, the *clip-clip* as he scored holes in each ticket while the plump teacher's smile remained fixed in her lipstick.

He took his time moving down the aisle. Reaching to take the ticket Ariana offered, he said, "A woman shouldn't be traveling in such a condition." He gauged the belly that spilled into her lap. "A bit risky, in my opinion. The wife has had five wee ones herself, and past the third month I don't let her out of the house."

"Yes, well," Ariana said, adjusting her bulk in the seat, "this trip is my mother's idea of fun. Quite a prankster. You're welcome to ask her about it if you care to have a chat. She's in the last car. You may find that the two of you have a great deal in common."

Her mother had died after a life of protracted bitterness and argument, meddling and manipulation. Believing that human lives tended to be shabby and in constant need of reform, she tried to shape anyone within reach. She had not allowed Ariana to choose schools, clothes, or morals. She had gone so far as to arrange a husband for her daughter, an accountant from the family shipyard, a decision that had sent Ariana packing, ultimately to Samoa without money or resources to return; meeting Miles had been her salvation. But even that precipitous flight had not cured her mother of her habitual intrusions. Near the end, with her breath coming in gasps through an oxygen mask, her mother had been issuing orders from her hospital bed in the study, not realizing that her daughter and son-in-law were fulfilling only those requests whose results she could see. Her instructions regarding the back lawn were heeded because the study window gave her an excellent view, but the rosebushes on the south side of the house, which flourished without her supervision, were allowed to grow wild, contrary to her wishes. Her son-in-law went to the barber when she told him to and stood up straight when she mentioned it, but he never removed his collection of box radios or the spare parts—the dead tubes, the tangled coils of wire, the cracked speaker cones—from the cellar workroom. What difference could it possibly make? "She's old and she's sick," he had said gently. "Let her believe what she wants."

All the more reason for Ariana to wonder why she was taking this trip just now. Her mother had written explicit instructions regarding the final disposal of her mortal remains: cremation, with her ashes sprinkled in the Willamette. A memorial stone to be placed in the rose garden. Two days before she died, however, she had a change of heart. She wished to be buried in a cemetery near Crater Lake. There was a resort there next to the cemetery, and Ariana was to escort the body. Crater Lake was only six hours by train. She extracted a promise, using frailty as a means of extortion. What was the sense of it? Was she suddenly frightened by the idea of cremation, the incineration of all that was left of the tangible self? If so, her own house was bordered on three sides by cemeteries. Jewish, Catholic, Protestant. She could have been buried in her own backyard, for all that it mattered, remaining a constant presence in the lives of those whom she had hounded and prodded for the past thirty years. But even in this last wish she had proved to be intractable and unreasonable, dictatorial and arbitrary.

In Salem four members of the state legislature boarded, as did six representatives for the timber industry and twelve loggers and their wives. The legislators and lobbyists arrived in various degrees of intoxication, while the loggers in their brown suits and ruler thin ties were as sober and disapproving as temperance workers. Their wives looked at the floor and disguised their chapped hands by clutching their purse straps. Although the lobbyists and legislators found seats immediately, the logging contingent bunched up in the aisle, a herd perplexed and clotted by choice, before moving on to the next car. When the loggers were gone, several bottles promptly began moving over seat backs and across the aisle, and one of the legislators began singing what Ariana recognized as a camp song but with obscene lyrics about the silver birch, beavers, and snow-capped mountain peaks. The conductor, not surprisingly, reappeared and helped himself to a drink here and a drink there. The more liquor was pressed upon him, the darker his face grew, and his mood became more jovial and more insinuating than before. After several long drafts from three different bottles, the conductor stumbled halfway down the length of the car, slumping into the seat across the aisle from Ariana's.

"Well, girlie," he said. "Well, if it isn't Mama with child." He rubbed his forehead with the resignation of one who knows the remedy will not provide the cure. His eyes looked glassy and swollen, as though he had been bitten by some venomous insect. His expressive eyebrows drooped. Ariana, who—even during her pregnancies—never traveled without a flask in her purse, recognized the signs. Her sympathies, however, were not engaged by his obvious discomfort; sowing and reaping, that was the way of nature. If he hadn't learned that lesson by now, he probably never would. Although she privately believed he should suffer in silence, she murmured the usual commonplace, wishing him a speedy return to health. "You're an understanding woman, I see, not holding a mistake here and there over a man's head. Your husband will be lucky in that, at least." He sighed and continued to massage his forehead and temples. "Allergies. I ought to know better."

"Yes," Ariana said, "you should."

In Eugene, when the plump, henna-haired home ec teacher and her pupils rose from their seats, the conductor jumped to his feet in a surprising show of recovery, and while they stood at the door waiting for the train to slow to a stop, he stroked the teacher's backside in full view of the legislators and lobbyists. The members of his private audience sniggered but kept their comments to themselves until the woman and her charges had been deposited on the platform. The teacher's set smile had not changed from the moment she entered the car to the second she set foot in the Eugene station, and Ariana wondered what sort of cost was involved: such bright artificiality in the face of such boorishness. Her mother, for instance, had always believed herself to be a cheerful person, possessed of a sunny disposition even in the stormiest weather, when in fact she had been a grump and a crab, a malcontent of the highest order. There had been enough psychic distance between the truth and the mask to kill a dozen beauty pageant hopefuls, much less embitter one old lady with emphysema; while waiting in the Eugene station, Ariana would not have been surprised to see the plump woman keel over and then be dragged away, the three girls carting her fleshy carcass from the platform, soldiers bearing their captain from the field of battle.

Two hours south of Eugene, the train struck three fully loaded log trucks at an unmarked crossing. The drivers, in a violent protest of certain pieces of failed safety legislation, had parked the trucks one next to the other and then retreated to the safety of the woods. They were not aware that a dozen of their own were aboard that particular train. One of the trucks had been doused with gasoline to ensure an explosion, and the resulting fireball ignited the trees lining the railbed as well as the logs that were littered like matchsticks along the tracks. Each car but the last flew off its wheels, tipped off the tracks, and fell onto its side like a toy. The impact, the darkness, the fires licking around the derailed cars caused their share of panic. Ariana could never be sure of the precise sequence of events. She hit her head, that much was clear, but on what or where? She was thrown about, then woke in the seats across the aisle from her own. Her nose was pressed against the window, her belly wedged into the gap between the back of one row and the seats of another. The air was filled with smoke, screaming could be heard in all directions, and Ariana tasted blood in her mouth while doubled over with cramps in her tiny space. She maneuvered herself around until she was standing on the interior wall of the train car, her head rising to the center of the aisle. She walked on the broken windows while the red glow of the fires danced in the windows above her head. Were there no others still on board? She seemed to be the only one left, though the screaming was still quite audible. Or was it she who was screaming? No, here was the state representative from Roseburg, there the grandmother whose pillbox hat the conductor had so recently complimented. Both were moaning, their eyes closed.

"Help me, please," the grandmother said through blood-caked lips. "I'm all alone."

Ariana patted her arm. "No. I'm here. But I need to get help."

"Yes, dear. Thank you."

"My legs are broke," the representative said, "my legs. I'm stuck."

They had been crushed in a twisted sandwich of seat backs. It would take a torch to remove him. "I'll find help," Ariana said, though she began to feel faint. She felt movement, a tremor running the length of her spine; black dots swam in front of her eyes. "I'm sure some sort of alarm has already gone out."

She could see the fires clearly now through the knuckle at the end of the car. How to get out? She was certainly in no condition to jump or to pull herself up, and it was doubtful that she could have scrambled to the opening even if she had not been pregnant and dazed. The car grew uncomfortably warm. She should have buried Cora Exley in one of the cemeteries next to the house, regardless of her mother's last capricious request, and then she would now be at home, asleep in her bed, threatened by nothing more than bad dreams. The air was stuffy and close, and each breath became more difficult, especially with that grip in her belly and back. Sleep. Sleep was the thing. A little rest would make everything right. Then she would see about the help they needed.

When she woke, she lay in thick grass underneath a giant fir many yards away from the fires, a blanket across her belly and legs. The drizzle had turned to rain, but the wind breathing from the fires was hot. She couldn't seem to stop coughing. Her face was streaked with wet ash. Through the smoke she could see constellations—Ursa Major, Ursa Minor, the faint winking of Cassiopeia. Dark shapes lay scattered about her on the grass. Other silhouetted figures, like illustrations from Dante, ran about the rail cars, one of which—the last car, the only one not derailed—had somehow ignited. She sat up, and her head threatened to fall from her shoulders, such was the headache, and her cough gave no sign of letting up. But thank goodness, the contractions, if that was what they were, seemed to have subsided.

"Ah, there you are, girlie. Up and about, are you?" The conductor stood in front of her, weaving like a punch-drunk boxer. Blood ran down the side of his face, he was coated in soot and char, and his eyes somehow seemed askew. "When we pulled you out, there was some question as to how much smoke you might have taken in. Coughing will do you a world of good, clear it out. Others in your car weren't so lucky, sorry to say. But all in all, everyone has behaved splendidly, splendidly. Real troopers, not a whiner in the lot of them. Well, there's still much to be done. Take care, girlie; there will be some medicos attending to you shortly, I'm sure."

It was not until he turned, his face illuminated again by the fire, that Ariana realized his eyebrows had vanished. She got to her feet, intending to follow, but she lost him immediately. The fires in the trees had been largely extinguished, but the baggage car was burning more fiercely than ever. Flames shot from the doorways and curled over the roof with a roar and the creaking of twisting metal. The firefighters were letting the car burn while making sure the flames didn't jump back into the woods. A tremendous hiss, a pop, and then a shower of sparks rising into the night sky like rockets, and everyone respectfully stepped back one more pace from the tracks.

"There she goes," said one of the firefighters, who was leaning on an axe. At first Ariana thought he was referring to her mother, whose body inhabited the coffin at the rear of the car. He meant the roof, however, and shortly thereafter flames began to rise upward with no more impediment than air. But in Ariana's mind, his comment would forever identify the moment when her mother was swallowed by the elements, connecting it to that hiss and pop, sounds that echoed in the dank woods, promising some sort of freedom and release. Even after her mother had been dead for more than ten years, Ariana Lambert would still feel her presence hovering nearby as a shower of sparks. No amount of killing, it seemed, would suffice; Cora Exley would haunt on, even if she were burned to cinders and her ashes scattered by wind and rain in the forest.

Ariana told this story to Claudia Montoya-Jones, her husband's older cousin, while the two of them sat on the back patio and enjoyed an unseasonably warm spring afternoon. Miranda Lambert, aged four months, slept in a wicker basket in the shade of an awning.

"A small fleet of ambulances, private cars, and pickups ferried the injured to Klamath Falls. As one of the least severe cases, I waited for space to become available in one of the cars. A woman wearing jeans and a western shirt drove up in a station wagon owned by the Shadow Crest Resort. Printed clearly on the front door panels, the logo of the resort—a blue lake, a campfire, and a forest—seemed in retrospect to be a mirror of our own scene. We jammed as many people together in the car as we could possibly fit—myself, the conductor, and the home economics teacher who had somehow reappeared.

Also two of her students and the grandmother with the pill-box hat. The woman—her name was Sharon—welcomed us, saying there was room for all of us at Shadow Crest. She hugged me particularly, knowing how difficult this whole business must be for me. I said that much as I wanted to see the resort, a stop at the hospital might be the first order of business. One of the conductor's eyes was badly crusted with blood, the grandmother's collarbone was broken, and the teacher had several parallel lacerations across her abdomen— her plum-colored skirt and white blouse had torn, each tear marked by blood as red as her lipstick. The conductor said there was no need of hospitals, however.

"'There, there, girlie,' he said. 'Don't you worry. Shadow Crest is quite renowned for its healing and restorative pow-ers. It beats a hospital twelve ways to Sunday.'

"By this time, however, my contractions had started again and were coming quite close together, and I felt as though a bowling ball hung between my legs. 'Time,' I said. I was gasping with pain but also from the *surprise* of how painful it was. 'I think it's time.'

"Sharon stopped the car on the shoulder of the highway and made me lie down on the seat while the conductor held a flashlight and the home ec teacher held my hand. Each con-traction was worse than the previous one. With Freddy there was the gas, and when I woke up the deed was done, but not with this one, and I thought to myself how horribly unfair it was. The home ec teacher removed her torn blouse and pro-ceeded to rip it into three pieces. One she gave me to bite when the pain was too great, another she gave to her stu-dents, who soaked it in the creek that ran parallel to the highway, then placed it on my forehead. The third she arranged between my legs for when the baby would arrive. She wore a girdle, but it could not hide the bulge of flesh that ringed her middle between her hips and her brassiere. 'We'll have you taken care of in a jiffy,' she said.

"'You're quite safe,' the conductor said, the light shaking in his hands.

"Then Sharon stooped between my legs and yelled, 'Push, goddamn it. Don't be such a princess.' She began to pull and tug while the conductor and the teacher encouraged my progress. Even the grandmother in the front seat, who was holding herself absolutely still because of her collarbone, gave me the reassurance of her years. Only the students were quiet, but I'm sure they were thinking that this was something they too would one day experience unless they were careful. When I was just past exhaustion, I felt Mira slide from me like a fish, and I wept for joy until I heard Sharon say there was nothing anybody could do, the baby must have been injured in the derailment. My body, she said as gently as possible, simply understood that the time had come to eliminate what could not be saved. She was so sorry, she said, first my mother and then my daughter."

Ariana raised her hands in exasperation. "Everything after that is a jumble. Picking up the pieces."

"So that's where it ends."

"Yes."

"And you say it's not a dream," Claudia Montoya-Jones said at last.

"No. Not a dream. There was nothing subordinate or shadowy about the experience. Miranda's birth certificate reads November 15, 1954. Born at St. Vincent's by caesarean. I can show you the scar, she was in the transverse position, and I thought she might never come out. But I have as clear a memory of her stillborn in the back seat of a station wagon on October 10, three days after my mother died. One has no more prominence than the other. Although I know that by objective standards my mother was cremated and her ashes scattered in the Willamette, I am equally sure that she was incinerated in her coffin in the back of a baggage car, the result of a labor protest in the woods. I am equally at home in both memories. This reality, of course, is by far the more pleasant of the two. But my existence here might simply indicate an unwillingness on my part to face the facts as they really are."

"Possibly. But I don't think so." Claudia Montoya-Jones sat back, her bracelets clanking against the metal arms of her chair. "There are the inconsistencies that might seem to be expressions of the psyche. The teacher and the students who leave the train in Eugene and are back again in time for the wreck. The conductor who drinks himself into a stupor, then jumps to his feet to fondle the home ec teacher. But I do not think it a dream either. How to account for that?"

"You're the mystic," Ariana said. *The nutcase*, she thought, *the loop-de-loop*. Ariana considered Claudia Montoya-Jones a crackpot and a loon, but Miles had convinced her to share her story while his cousin was visiting, and although she had initially resisted telling something so intimate to a relative stranger, she found Claudia Montoya-Jones a good listener, whatever else she might be. The story poured from her. And even though she harbored no hope that the older woman would provide a more satisfactory explanation than her analyst, she did feel a sense of unburdening that had previously escaped her. She expected Claudia Montoya-Jones to be shocked, but Ariana's story was not surprising to her at all. It was red meat in her mouth.

Claudia Montoya-Jones sat poised in her patio chair, her ringed fingers clicking away on her glass of iced tea. Even into her fifties some faint patina of the starlet she had once been hung about her. Her hair carried hints of Doris Day, her dancer's legs bobbed in capris, but a mandala swung between her breasts. "Ever since I can remember I've had the sense that my life is not my *only* life," Ariana said. *Why, oh why, am I talking about this to you?* "I was hoping you could explain it."

It was then, however, that Freddy chose to wake from his nap, which woke his sister, and Miles appeared in his barbecue apron to ask where in blazes was the charcoal, and Ariana never did receive the answer to her question. Freddy was impossible, shouting whenever one of the adults attempted to pick him up, Mira chose that moment to be hungry, and Ariana's breasts drooped with a sudden load of milk, staining a blouse she had purchased only the day before. Miles, who was not a very handy cook, had a devil of a time with the briquettes and the lighter fluid; after several dousings with little smoke and less flame, he threw a match into the puddle below the charcoal, and his eyebrows curled and sizzled. A time or two during their dinner of scorched hamburgers, Claudia Montoya-Jones seemed anxious to renew the conversation, but some essential barrier had been erected and Ariana's initial reluctance was once again restored. She had seriously begun to question her sanity, and a counseling session with Madame Claudia, Seer to the Stars, hardly seemed like the gateway to mental health. The older woman had been too quick to embrace the notion of an alternative reality for her taste. Ariana had hoped, frankly, for more skepticism.

In the past Ariana had dismissed such episodes as imagination run amok, the effect of too much alcohol, too much flight from her mother. Since her days in Samoa she had chosen to organize her days in such compulsive order as not to allow a misstep. But since Miranda's birth, the tug of other threads, other realities, had grown impossibly strong. Her life—filled with choices previously denied her—was becoming more slippery each second. Instead of making one choice and leaving all others behind, she had the delicate task of sorting through the multiple strands of possibility that posed a future but also, for her, marked a past. Each instant had become tenuous; never knowing when she might slip into the lockstep of another life determined by choices she could have made or might have made, she held on to the material nature of the present moment with the urgency of someone reaching for a banister in a dark stairwell.

Shortly after midnight, she slipped from bed to check on Mira. She was careful not to disturb Miles, who had had a tough evening, what with the barbecue and the lighter fluid. His forehead was red and raw and coated in Mira's baby oil. She found her robe in a heap on the floor and struggled to put it on; when she opened Mira's door, she saw her daughter sleeping peacefully. Mira was on her stomach and knees, her face pressed against the slats of her crib. Her nightlight drew stripes across the bedclothes. Ariana quietly closed the door and crawled back into bed as though she were falling into a pit of feathers. When she woke at eight, however, she felt hollow and sluggish, and the clock mocked her fatigue. "Rock-a-Bye, Baby" echoed in her head with the persistence of a cigarette song. In the kitchen, Miles was pouring coffee for his cousin. Claudia Montoya-Jones wore a kimono, the silk scarf she used to protect her hair at night, and her ever-present bracelets and rings.

"You see, Miles, what did I tell you? She's exhausted." She held Ariana at arm's length. "What do men know about babies? They sleep and sleep, they never listen, and they pretend nothing's wrong because they don't hear anything."

"I didn't," Miles said. "If I don't hear anything, I'm not responsible, am I?"

"Very selective, his hearing." She rubbed Ariana's back with a practiced hand. "He doesn't hear his daughter, he doesn't hear you get up or when you're singing her to sleep, and he doesn't wake up any of the countless times it happens during the night. I don't know, sweetheart, he's my family, but sometimes the dumb cluck is as obtuse as a stone."

Yes, what could Miles know? He slept unaware of the dangers that lurked between each tick of the clock. His forehead, burned last night, gleamed pink this morning as though he were the picture of health. Ariana stood in the middle of the kitchen, turning as though she had never seen this room before, unable to recognize the patterns of light falling across the table, the coffee cups, the juice glasses, the plates with their pieces of toast. She looked first to her husband and then to her husband's cousin as she held her daughter on her shoulder, not knowing when or in what life she had picked Miranda up.

6
STRAWBERRIES

Unable to sleep at four o'clock one Saturday morning, I found Mr. Lambert playing solitaire in the cellar workroom. He was surrounded by his entire collection of box radios, but the radios were silent. Instead, the wind-up phonograph was playing the opera I had heard him play over and over again. The moment was frozen but not without sound: the recording was tinny, the record scratched, and the phonograph an antique, but he listened with the rapt concentration of a blind man, the two of clubs dangling between one finger and thumb. It threatened to slip out of his hand as the moments passed, but then he yawned, saw me in the doorway, and placed the deuce over the ace.

"Fish! Awake? It's the middle of the night. I didn't wake you, did I? Music too loud?"

There were strange sounds aplenty in the Lambert house, due in part to its age, the creakings and groanings of an old house, but due in larger measure to its occupants. *Madama Butterfly* or *La Bohème,* for instance, might be wailing at any hour of the day or night.

"That's okay; I couldn't sleep."

"Ariana couldn't either," he yawned again, "so neither could I. She's mowing the grass."

I heard the faint growl of the lawn mower moving toward, then away from, the house. Mr. Lambert had attached a headlight to the front of the mower, and it was not unusual for Mrs. Lambert to be outside two or three nights a week during decent weather. The beam of her headlight went back and forth, back and forth, sweeping across the first-floor windows at every turn. The Lamberts had an enormous lawn, a series of three terraces, and if she had tried to mow it all at once she would have been at it for seven or eight hours. Fortunately, the closest neighbors were the residents of the three cemeteries bordering the Lambert property, and they were not fussy about noise at night. After three hours of mowing, she would come in at dawn, dead on her feet, her cotton nightgown soaked in dew and sweat, able finally to sleep for an hour or two. Mr. Lambert had tried on several occasions to hire a gardener, but she vetoed the notion each time it was raised. He accused her of having stock in Briggs & Stratton.

"Has she ever tried warm milk?"

"She's just one of those people who are afraid to close their eyes. They're afraid of what might happen in the blink."

"Like what?"

He shrugged and lifted the needle off the record, and the cellar became quiet. "The world might be different; she might be different. She might wake up and discover that she's an old maid living alone in a drafty house. Or a bitter old woman who couldn't get out of bed without nursing some sort of grudge against her family. She knows it's silly, but she doesn't feel like taking any chances either."

I didn't understand any more than I had before, but I did recognize that Mr. Lambert was reluctant to say more.

"She could tie herself to a bedpost," I offered. "Or to you. Use a piece of string. Then if she started to get scared she could give the string a little tug. Remind herself where she is. Who and what she's connected to."

His laugh was a dry bark. "I'll have to suggest that. Show her who the true master is, that it?" He looked at the game of solitaire on the workbench, then swept the cards into a pile. "I can't even cheat and win," he muttered. "Listen, let's wake up the guys, take a little trip. We'll be spontaneous. What do you think?"

"Okay by me."

"Fine. Let's do it. Wake 'em up, will you? I'll load the car."

I went upstairs. Freddy's room was empty, the bed unslept in. He had passed through my room sometime after midnight, using the window for an exit, and had not yet returned. What was I supposed to say to his father? Mira was another matter. Her room was at the top of a dilapidated staircase, and every tread announced my arrival. I found the switch near the door and squinted in the sudden light. A mound of sheets and blankets had been piled in the center of her double bed, and the pile kept time with her breathing.

"Mira," I said, "your dad wants to go for a drive. Come on, get up."

The pile shook. "No. Go away. Sky dark. White girl wantum sleep."

"Come on, Mira. I think he's lonely. Your mom's pushing the lawn mower around and Freddy's off somewhere. We're it."

"No."

"Please?"

103

"Go away."

"Not until you get up."

She sat up, her hair disheveled, her nightgown falling off one narrow shoulder. "I'm up. Now go away."

"Come on, Mira."

"What time is it, anyway?"

"A little after four, I think."

"What is he thinking?"

"He says he wants to be spontaneous."

"You mean just because Mom can't sleep, the rest of us have to enlist."

"I guess so. I couldn't sleep either."

"Jeez," she laughed, "I must be the only normal one in the house."

This was good coming from her: her posture had become rigid, her shoulders squared, her head cocked as though she were listening to a message only she could hear. She could find a spiritual presence in anything, including old toenails.

"Okay," she said, "so it's important. Tell Dad I'll be down directly. After I fluff up a bit."

In the kitchen, Mr. Lambert was bent over a picnic basket, filling it with bags of potato chips and pretzels, Twinkies and Ding-Dongs. An ice chest the size of a steamer trunk sat in the middle of the kitchen floor. With its lid off, the chest looked big enough to hide a body. "Crack some ice into that, will you, Fish?"

"Mira's getting dressed," I said, "but I couldn't get Freddy up." Not a lie, strictly speaking.

He straightened himself with an effort. "Late night, I guess. Or has he flown the coop? Has our Freddy gone AWOL?"

"I wouldn't put it like that."

"Stepped out, maybe. Just for a second."

"Maybe," I said. "I guess that's it."

"My Freddy," he sighed, speaking to the air. "We'll have to have a talk. Pounding nails and stacking firewood must not be enough. Obviously."

Mira pushed through the swinging door and took a good look at the basket her father was loading. "Lordy, there's more preservatives than food here. Eat too much of this stuff and your joints will lock up, never to bend again."

Other than getting dressed in a pair of shorts, tee shirt, and sandals, I'm not sure what she had done to get herself ready. There were rats in her hair the size of softballs and her cheek still carried the creases from her pillow, but her eyes were bright behind her glasses, two moons in a predawn sky. Her backpack was slung over one shoulder, and it bulged with the rectangular shapes of books.

"Wherever we're going, let's get this show on the road."

Mr. Lambert stopped throwing things into his basket for one moment. "I thought we'd head for the island, watch the sunrise from the houseboat."

"And pick some strawberries? They have the best fields on the island, Fish."

"We can pick some if you want," her father said. "But no more than an hour's worth. I'm not going to get heat exhaustion for a bunch of berries."

"Okay, okay. We'll go before it gets hot. You don't even have to pick, Dads, just take us." She handed me a jug for ice water. "Let's get this stuff into the car so we get there before noon. I think he's packed every artificial food group known to Dow."

I picked up the hamper and headed toward the door just as Mrs. Lambert came through from the outside. Her nightgown was soaked to her knees. Blades of grass were plastered to her feet. She had a flashlight with her, and she pointed it at each of our faces.

"Oh, god," she cried, "who died? Who was it? What else could you be up to at this hour?"

Mira and I crawled into the back of Mr. Lambert's Buick, where she promptly fell asleep with a paperback open on one leg, her knee marking her place. We were traveling in the tunnel of the Buick's headlights, the dark ribbon of the river on our right, Forest Park looming above us on our left. The horizon to the east had changed from black to deep blue, and Mr. Lambert was pushing the old car to beat the sun.

"The houseboat is nothing special," Mr. Lambert was saying to me. He looked into the rearview mirror as though that might help me hear above the racket of the Buick's suspension and fenders, which seemed in imminent danger of falling off. "Just a roof and a raft, really. But it's been in Mrs. Lambert's family ever since her grandfather won his first contract with the navy. So we keep it, and if we use it once a summer, we've had a big year."

"I'll bet it's pretty nice."

"You'll see."

He turned off the highway onto a narrow bridge, slowing as we rose to the top of the green metal span.

"I found something yesterday I thought you might be interested in," Mr. Lambert said. The Buick tipped down as we crossed the peak of the bridge, and he handed a snapshot with scalloped edges over the seat back. In the watery light of the false dawn I could barely make out the figure of my mother, wearing a corsage and gloves and standing next to the awkward shape of Miles Lambert—a scarecrow in a suit with wide lapels, the shoulder pads the size of wings. That my mother and Mr. Lambert had once been engaged was an old story, but the picture somehow turned that story from family lore into the present tense.

"We went to my cousin's wedding four days before I started work for the navy. Your mother insisted we have a picture made since the photographer was right there. 'What's the big deal?' your mother says. 'He's shooting five rolls. He can take one more shot.' Your mother is quite a girl."

With the instinct of a cat, Mira woke up just as the Buick nosed into the space in front of the rickety dock to which the houseboat had been secured. Gravel crunched underneath the tires, and the hull of the car rocked to a stop. I had not been able to pull my eyes away from the picture of my mother and Mr. Lambert.

"What time is it?" Mira asked.

"A couple minutes past five," Mr. Lambert said.

"Boy-oh-brother, what a lousy dream I just had. Phew." She stretched and punched me in the ribs. "So what's the matter with you, Fisheroo?"

"Nothing." I slipped the snapshot into my shirt pocket and opened my door.

The houseboat rocked in its moorings as we stepped aboard. The deck echoed hollowly under our feet. Mr. Lambert had not been guilty of excessive modesty—the houseboat was nothing much, even to my uncritical eye. A ladder rose up one exterior wall to the roof, which served as a deck. Inside, the single room was a plywood box, and the furnishings were definitely of the camp variety: a couple of cots, folding chairs, a stack of wool blankets, a collapsible camp stove. A lantern hung from a wire, its glass chimney brown with soot. The boat had never been hooked up to the power lines that ran ten yards from the dock; Mrs. Lambert, in whose name the houseboat was listed, had rejected electrical service, saying it would be a pathetic disguise of what was so obviously shabby and low rent.

"Pretty nasty, huh?" Mira said.

"No," I said, "it's okay. It's pretty neat actually that there's nothing here."

"You think so?"

"Sure."

"Okay, then, let's go do some strawberries."

She handed me a couple of buckets from a stack in one corner and took two for herself. "Let's go, Dad."

Mr. Lambert came in with the cooler, set it down, then fished out a can of beer. His face was gray with fatigue. He covered his eyes. "I'm not feeling so hot. You two go ahead. I think I'll sit upstairs. Watch the light come up. I'm about to fall apart."

"Poor Dads." She looked closely at him. "We'll stick around while you take a little nap."

"No, no. Don't do that. Get out there and get us some berries, all right?"

"You sure?" She looked into his eyes once again, shook her head, then shrugged. "Okay, let's hike."

"No, here," he handed Mira a set of keys, "take the car. You shouldn't run into anything. Come back in the next couple of hours, will you?"

"We'll be back in a jiffy."

We both crowded into the front seat, though there was barely room enough for one amidst the boxes of radio parts. Mira seemed to know what to do with the clutch and the three-speed transmission. Practice in the Lambert driveway was my guess. She backed out and headed down the narrow two-lane without too much lurching and only one blast of backfire.

"Good job, Miss Andretti."

Mira cranked down the window and turned the knob on the radio. "Paperback Writer" bloomed inside the car, then blew out the window. We were taking off; Mira might have been doing all of thirty-five miles an hour. Orange bands of light streaked the eastern horizon. Mira cut the headlights, and we could have been submariners, the light liquid and shifting. The narrow road served as a dike between the fields that stretched out below us; near one dark field we rolled to a stop along the narrow shoulder next to a leaning shed that advertised STRAWBERRYS in dripping red paint.

We scrambled down the slope, then set to work in adjacent rows. Mira assured me that the owner of the field was an old family friend and would not mind our being here at dawn. "We'll just leave a couple of bucks on the counter," she said, "and I'll write a note."

The berries were small but red all the way through, firm without being woody. And very, very sweet.

"Behold," she said, holding one of the berries like a specimen, "*Fragaria chiloensis*—indigenous to Chile and the western half of North America, undoubtedly a descendant of those plants cultivated by the Multnomah five hundred years ago. They're like clockwork, the way they call to me. But,

Fishbait, if you eat them all here, we won't have any to take home."

"I'll pick my share," I said. "I'm allowing my appetite to express itself in a healthy and vital manner. My astral body is expressing joy and oneness with nature." I had been around Mira long enough to know that most of what she knew had been memorized from one of her father's many outdated sets of encyclopedias. I also knew enough of her spacey theosophical jargon to needle her. It was starting to become a bit too familiar.

"Very funny. You shouldn't make fun of what you don't understand. One of these days you'll wake up feeling like an idiot."

"I don't need theosophy for that."

We picked our rows on our knees in silence. Our shadows stretched across the ground. Ever since their side trip to Czechoslovakia, I had been waiting for some word from my mother or father about the improved state of their marriage. Instead, I received an inventory of their latest purchases: cuckoo clocks and pewterware and a *schrank* of heavy Bavarian wood that would cost a fortune to ship. I kept waiting for them to take their summer as seriously as I was.

"Dad gave you the picture, didn't he?" Her buckets were full, and she stood stretching in what had become the full light of day, while I had picked little more than half a bucket, with the end nowhere in sight. "I wasn't asleep the whole time," she said. "Besides, I've seen it before. Ten years ago I clogged the downstairs toilet when I tried to flush Dad's overcoat. He was about to leave for a business meeting downtown, and I thought if he didn't have a coat he wouldn't be able to go. He would stay at home and play pick-up sticks or Candyland with me. One sleeve went down before the coat clogged the drain, but the water kept running and running and ruined the oriental rugs in three rooms. In the cellar Dad's books were swollen the size of pumpkins. He was sloshing through the water, moving his stuff where it was dry, when he pulled out that picture from the back of one of his radios. He looked at it for a long time. I was sitting on the cellar steps, watching him because I felt so lousy, everything was such a mess. I asked him who the woman was. 'I could have married her,' he said, 'but then where would we be?'"

"You wouldn't have been born," I said. "Me either."

"That's just it. You're wrong. So was Dads. His decision didn't determine a thing. We're just souls looking for bodies, so if there hadn't been a Miranda Lambert, there would have been a Trixie Lemieux or a Richard Agincourt. And that's where I would have been. Different name, different body, but the same soul. The same me."

"Jesus, Mira, you're the weirdest girl of all time."

A pair of herons lounging in the channel suddenly rose from the water with a rush of wings, their blue necks folded back on their shoulders, their bills pointed toward the sun.

"Well, what do you think we did before we were born? Do you think we didn't exist? You think your mother and father could have meant the difference between Fish and not-Fish? We've all been busy little souls, I hope to tell you; we've lived a couple hundred lifetimes at least."

"No wonder I'm so tired all the time."

"Don't joke. You were probably a riverboat captain on the Mississippi in 1875 and a galley slave for the Romans. My guess is that you were always close to water."

"Just because I fell in once?"

"Spiritual attractions run throughout the lifetime of a soul, regardless of the body you inhabit. You fell in because it was your nature to stare at the element that attracts you. If you had been born to parents in the middle of Death Valley, you would have fallen into the kitchen sink just for some relief. I've always been at home on this island; every time I come here it feels like the echo of another life, and every time I eat one of these berries, there is no time. I nearly lose myself."

There was no arguing with Mira once she had an idea in her head. Theosophy was Mira's way of categorizing and controlling the universe. She was welcome to it. Parts of it made sense to me, while other parts seemed like the wackiest sort of imaginings. I picked strawberries and let her rattle on, the words washing over my head like the flow from a garden hose or the noise of one of her father's opera recordings. If I wasn't merely the product of my father and mother's coupling, then what was I? There were certain things about my parents that I disliked: my father's forced heartiness, my mother's spontaneity that seemed to me more manufactured than genuine. Their mutual profligacy when it came to their finances. According to Mira, I ought to have been rejoicing in the theosophist perspective that I was not automatically heir to the traits I found objectionable. But on the whole I preferred to think that the enemies within myself might be more kindly rationalized by heredity. That seemed less demoralizing than the notion of making the same mistakes over and over again for centuries, with only the slightest improvements to show for the effort.

Freddy's Mustang was parked in the space in front of the houseboat when Mira and I returned, and Freddy and Gale

Lewis were asleep on the houseboat floor, naked, without the benefit even of a sheet or blanket. Strewn about the floor were their clothes, a parody of passion, haste, and frenzy. Buttons were missing, fabric was torn. A used Trojan drooped off the edge of the ice chest like a Dali clock. Tanned to the waist from his summer construction job, Freddy looked all the more naked for the demarcation of pale and dark skin. When Mira nudged Freddy in those tan ribs, he grinned but kept his eyes screwed shut.

"For crying out loud, Freddo. Why don't you just do it on the Burnside Bridge? Let everyone have a look."

"Hey, Sis." His voice was slurred, singsong, an accent of smoke and vapors. "The Fish-man with you?"

"I'm here," I said. I couldn't help admiring Gale Lewis's brown curves, which reminded me of Amanda Baird and the curves I was no longer welcome to see. Gale curled around Freddy, using him like a fan dancer's props.

"Where's Dad?" Mira said, throwing a blanket over their braided legs. "He was going to lie down on the roof when we left."

"Dunno. Only thing we saw was the ice chest and the basket. We thought we'd catch a few winks before you came back from picking those big ol' berries you always have a hankering for." He seemed about to fall asleep in midsentence. "We're wrecked, you know. Thought all of you went down the road. Didn't mean to offend. You did pick strawberries, didn't you?"

"What else is there to do out here? Dad gave us the keys, told us to go ahead, he was going to lie down on the roof and drink a beer. That's what he said, didn't he, Fish? He was going to lie down on the roof and watch the sunrise. He looked lousy." She put a foot on his shoulder and stepped down until he opened his eyes. "Give it to me straight. What's the matter with you?"

He shook his head back and forth as though she were beating him. "Nothing, Sis, I swear. Pure sweaty fatigue, you know. Who gave you the keys?"

"Dad, who else?"

"Mira behind the wheel. Oh, Jesus."

Gale Lewis began to giggle. "He's so so tired," she laughed, "because he worked so hard." *Ha, ha, ha.*

"Bitch," Freddy said.

"My little man."

Mira grabbed a handful of her own hair. "Great golly Ned." She ignored Gale, and focused her attention on her brother.

"Well, if you're not too tired and not too stupid, you can help us find him. Okay? Can you do that?"

"Sure, sure. Don't worry. He's taking a walk or watching the birds. Don't get so bent out of shape."

But Mira was unconvinced. Some alarm had gone off, something had persuaded her that all was not as it should be. We threw their clothes into a pile and helped them as they stumbled into underwear and tee shirts and shorts. They kept falling down and laughing like hyenas until Mira had had enough.

"Oh, what was I thinking?" she said. "Forget it, Freddy. Go dunk your head in the channel, why don't you? Come on, Fish."

We piled back into the car. "We shouldn't have left him. Damn it, damn it, damn it." She pounded the steering wheel as the starter cranked and cranked. When the engine finally roared into life, Mira popped the clutch, gravel sprayed into the wheel wells, and the engine died.

"Take it easy," I said. "No matter how stoned Freddy is, it's probably like he said. Your dad's off doing dad things. Just slow down, okay?"

"What do you know?" She was more careful this time, however. The engine roared, but she let the clutch out slowly, the car shivered from front to rear, and we backed away from the houseboat.

Our search did not take long; we spotted him within a half-mile—the pendulum-long angles of his neck and shoulders, the sharp points of his elbows, knees, and throat. He sat on the shoulder of the road, surveying the expanse of strawberries, his white hair a flare among all that green. A family of ducks splashed in the puddles at the head of the rows.

"See," I said, "Freddy was right after all."

"Thank god for that."

Mira slowed to a stop on the wrong side of the road and rolled down the window.

"Hey, Dads," she said, "what're you doing? We were worried when you weren't on the boat."

He gave no indication that he had heard other than a slow turning of his giant's head.

"Jesus god," Mira breathed. "Jesus. Just look at him."

Mira became an experienced driver that morning, and I have never been half so frightened of anything since. Together we tugged and prodded Mr. Lambert to his feet, then pushed him into moving toward the back seat of the car. The right side of his face had fallen, his right arm was limp, and his right foot dragged with each step. A thread of saliva ran from the downturned corner of his mouth. Viewed only from the right, he was a dead man, but his left eye expressed a wry desperation—*wouldn't you know it*—and gratitude that we had come. He seemed interested in the mechanics of the situation, how we were going to manage things. He tried to speak, but he could only produce a noise that sounded like strangulation. We pushed him through the open back door, and he slumped across the length of the seat. Mira got the Buick moving once again, wondered aloud whether to stop at the houseboat to tell Freddy, then decided against it. What could he have done besides fall down or fall asleep while Gale Lewis cackled like a hen? We passed the Mustang and the gravel parking space, and she stepped on the balky accelerator.

The bridge to the island was narrow, and that's where we had our first scare. Mira was taking no chances of sideswiping the bridge, so she took the whole road, our wheels straddling the center line. Which worked out well enough until a garbage truck turned into the opposing lane. She pulled the Buick over just in time, but it was a mere foretaste of what was to come. There was the log truck on Highway 30, a Cadillac on 23rd, and an ambulance in the emergency room driveway of Good Samaritan. Every driver, without exception, glared at Mira and me and yelled curses we couldn't hear. Her mouth set, Mira gripped the steering wheel fiercely, guiding the ancient green car as best she could while it doddered along at forty miles an hour. Without her father at the wheel, I expected tires to fall off, the brakes to fail, or the engine to give up the ghost entirely. In the back seat Mr. Lambert breathed heavily, making that strangling sound every now and again. "It's okay, Dads. We'll get everything sorted out," Mira said. "You just hang in there. Leave the rest to me. To Fish and me."

She talked to her father throughout the trip. The only pause in her reassuring tone came when she was struggling to avert some new disaster on the roadway. It wasn't until we reached the hospital that I saw a break in her composure. Her father had been loaded onto a gurney, and Mira was answering the admitting clerk's questions. The clerk was called away from her desk for a moment, and Mira began to tremble.

"It's my fault," she said. "I didn't listen to what I saw, and I shouldn't have left him. His aura was practically crackling. What goddamn good is it if you don't listen?"

"Cut it out, Mira. He told us to go."

"It's so easy for you," she said bitterly. "Things happen and you're never responsible. I'm telling you, his head was on fire."

I had never before seen water spurt from someone's eyes; she covered her eyes with her hands and water fell from between her fingers. Tears coursed down Mira's face, running in dusty trails down her cheeks and falling from her chin. I handed her a box of tissues, unable to think of what to say.

"Maybe I should go," I said. "I could find a phone and call your mother."

"That's a sensible thought," she said, blowing her nose, blotting her eyes and face. "Tell her to bring someone with a driver's license, will you? So we can move that junk heap of Dad's."

Mrs. Lambert made it to the hospital in record time; she and Mira fell into each other's arms, but she had no interest in falling apart. She checked first at the nurses' station, where she was told she would have to wait for the doctor. Tests were being performed. Samples needed to be analyzed. Her husband was comfortable. But further information could come only from the doctor himself.

Mrs. Lambert stamped her foot. "This is not acceptable. I want to see my husband, and I want to see his doctor. Immediately."

The nurse was sorry. She had no control over the doctor's agenda.

"I hate doctors," Mrs. Lambert said. "They act like god, only less communicative and more condescending."

We sat for two hours. The waiting area filled with the aged, the poor, and children with broken bones and bloody homemade bandages. A janitor swept under our feet and dumped the ashtrays into plastic garbage sacks. Mira told her mother what had happened, omitting any mention of Freddy or Gale Lewis. Her father, she said, didn't appear to be in pain.

"But he looked terrible, Mom, like," Mira's forehead wrinkled in concentration, "like a wreck. A train wreck." She looked around the room as though there might be someone waiting to contradict her. "I don't know why I said that."

Mrs. Lambert held her daughter's hand. "You poor kids. You've had a tough day, but Miles is going to be fine, I'm sure of it. In another time, he's still doing navy calisthenics, so you're not to worry. You understand me? Fish?"

"I'm okay."

"You're sure?"

"I'm sure."

"Oh, my god." She clapped her hand over her mouth. "I just now realized. Mira. Mira drove. You drove. How else could you get here? Oh, baby, I don't know where my mind is. You told me, but you know how your mind can get stuck.

118

What was I thinking? Good lord, what a fool. Thank god you weren't killed."

"I did pretty well," Mira said. "We got here."

"What I'd like to know," Mrs. Lambert said, "is where your brother has been all this time."

"Well," Mira said, "he stopped by the houseboat a little while before we found Dads, but we haven't seen him since."

"What was he doing besides running around with Gale?"

"The usual, I guess." Mira looked at me, looking for help. "I don't know."

"He said something about a workout," I said.

"Right," Mira said. "That's right."

"And I almost believe you. But I'll take your word for it."

A nurse pushed through the swinging door that led from the treatment areas. "Mrs. Lambert?" she said. "Dr. Caselli has a moment." She motioned to the brightly lit hallway behind the door. "Back this way, please."

"Tell you what, kids," Mrs. Lambert said, pulling her wallet from her purse, "why don't you take a break in the cafeteria? I'll meet you there in half an hour or so. After the high-and-mighty speaks with the peasantry."

She handed Mira a five-dollar bill.

"Go ahead. I need to talk to this guy, and I might have to get mean. I'd rather not have you witness it."

"All right, Mom."

Mrs. Lambert followed the nurse into the bowels of the emergency room while we went the opposite direction, following the signs through a rabbit warren of hallways to the cafeteria. Nurses in starched whites barreled past us. In one hallway, an old man lay on a gurney, his eyes wide open, staring at the pinholes in the ceiling.

In the cafeteria a blue haze of cigarette smoke and grease drifted through the air while a squadron of old women in hairnets gave orders to the high school girls who cleared the tables and did the dishes.

"You want anything?" Mira asked.

"No."

"Me neither. I guess we just hang out for a while."

"I guess."

Adjacent to the cafeteria was a small patio. At tables shaded by umbrellas, a few clerks ate their lunches. We found a spot, but Mira could not sit still. She crossed her legs and her top leg began to bounce; she uncrossed her legs and her knees began to jiggle.

"I can't stand this. I've got to do something."

"Like what?"

"I don't know. Call home, maybe, or Gale's. See if dopey Freddy is back on the planet. Mom is going to kill him if he doesn't show up. You have some dimes?"

I gave her what was in my pockets. "I'll wait here."

"Back in a sec."

In the shade of the umbrellas the patio was pleasant. A breeze played with the fringes of the umbrellas, and the ferns in the planters bounced in time to the air. I wished I had a book with me; even one of Mira's theosophy tracts would have been okay. Anything to keep from thinking about Mira's father, the way his face had gone half dead, half alive. In my shirt pocket the snapshot of my mother and Mr. Lambert tingled. The colors were faded, but my mother's eyes were clear, as were the points of Mr. Lambert's lapels. In another world, I thought, my mother and Mr. Lambert had married, my father serving as best man. And in that other world Mira and I were drifting, waiting for invitations yet to come.

Freddy answered Mira's phone call with the news that he'd run the Mustang into a guardrail on Front Avenue. The car still ran, but one fender was missing and the left front wheel had a distinct wobble. He and Gale Lewis had stiff necks, she had a bruise the shape of Rhode Island on her right arm, and he could barely put weight on his left ankle. He had hit his head on the steering wheel. But when he heard about his father, he promised to come. He'd take the bus if he had to.

Following her conference with the doctor, Mrs. Lambert found us on the patio. The news was neither good nor bad. Mr. Lambert was in intensive care, he was comfortable and resting, but the doctor could not be precise about his recovery. Suspecting an embolism, Dr. Caselli had ordered anticoagulants, but there was no way to know how long Mr. Lambert might be in the ICU, nor was there any way to know the degree to which his speech or coordination might remain affected. The doctor was optimistic but guilty of bad jokes. He reassured Mrs. Lambert by saying that she would be slapping away the big galoot's hands sooner than she could imagine. Mrs. Lambert had seen the big galoot: he was sleeping, there was a tube up his nose and another in his arm, and his hands weren't going anywhere anytime soon.

I was to have my own concerns. Freddy showed up an hour after Mira's phone call, his hair still wet from a shower. He was limping, an adhesive bandage held his forehead together, and his eyes were clear but as red-rimmed as a wound. An aerogram addressed to me with a Strasbourg postmark had been delivered that morning, and Freddy was good

enough to bring it along. The misshapen handwriting be-
longed to my mother, who wrote only when she could not
avoid it. I quickly scanned the letter, looking for the high-
lights, and I must have blanched. "What's the matter,
Fisheroo?" Mira asked.

"Nothing," I said. "Mom says they're tired of Europe.
They're coming home. I think they're coming home."

During the next few days I must have reread the letter
twenty or thirty times just to be sure I had read it correctly.
No matter how many times I read the letter and looked at the
snapshot of my mother and Mr. Lambert, I never saw anything I recognized.

August 16, 1968
Dear Fish,

*Well, here's the news. There's no nice way to tell you: your father and
I are calling it quits. I know you won't be happy about this, but life will
go on.*

*We came to Europe thinking we could work things out. But Europe is
nothing but museums and castles, cathedrals and historical markers. I am
so sick of it I could die. The Germans and French are a bunch of hypocrites
and fools, if you ask me. They set all kinds of store by history and tradi-
tion, but there's no one like a European for blowing it up first opportunity
he gets. When I get home, it will take three men and a boy just to get me
out of Bullock's. And then only after I've bought something sleazy and
cheap. Blah, blah, blah.*

*It was the cathedral here in Strasbourg that was the final touch. For
me, anyway. They have quite a gimmick, an astronomic clock, a copy of
one first installed in 1352 (trust me, it was on the back of one of your father's postcards). Don't ask me why a church should be famous for a clock,
but there's Europe in a nutshell. Where anything can be good so long as it's*

old. On the hour you get all sorts of hoo-hah—the Twelve Apostles, roosters, you name it. I watched the way this clock-in-a-church diced up the time with all this Old World precision and fussiness, and I thought, Time is marching, sister, and you've got nowhere to go.

Your father digs the clock in a big way, all those gears and pulleys, he's like Miles in that regard, but it depressed the hell out of me. Still does, just thinking about it.

This seems very familiar somehow. And very sad. I'm sorry about it. Twenty years ago, I wrote Miles a Dear John, told him about your father and me. Now I'm writing another one care of the Lamberts, only this time it's to you. Sorry sorry sorry.

7

ADAGIO,
1958

It is August, and the Beckers have finally arrived!

Miles Lambert throws open the massive front door to
greet his best friends from home, Alan and Sylvia Becker. It
has been too long, five years, since their last visit. At first
nothing seems to have changed. As always, while the cabbie
pulls their bags from the trunk, Alan and Sylvia stand in the
circular driveway as though shipwrecked, staring at the out-
lines of this enormous home with a look that is frank with
envy. Brick, Tudor, half-timbered; the turrets and gargoyles,
the steeply pitched slate roof. Miles, that dog, married
money, and his wife inherited the whole kit and kaboodle. So
Alan and Sylvia stare as always, but this time there is a new
face at their knees: their four-year-old son, Calvin, nick-
named Fish for an episode last year when he fell into a koi
pond and almost drowned. The boy is pudgy, his knees are
dimpled, and his arms still bear a crease across each forearm
from baby fat. Confronted by this huge castle of a house inhabited by people he has never met, he is lost and popeyed.
He clings to his mother's legs and buries his head in her skirt.

Miles's children, six-year-old Freddy and four-year-old

Mira, crowd around the newcomer, making his fright even more profound, until their mother gently shoos them away. At a mere five feet Ariana, unlike Miles, does not tower over children. At a distance she could be mistaken for one of them. Her voice is soft, quiet, not one of those high-pitched voices adults cultivate especially for children. She speaks no differently to her children than she does to her husband; Freddy and Mira behave simply because she refuses to raise her voice. There can be no competing noise if one is to hear what she has to say.

"There are cookies in the kitchen," she is saying now, "and you're welcome to have some. If Freddy and Mira haven't finished them off already, the little pigs. Wouldn't you like to come? Have a little snack?" She holds her hand out, and Fish slowly disengages from his mother's legs and skirt and allows himself to be towed away.

"Miles," Sylvia cries, breaking the moment of silence that follows the withdrawal of Ariana and the children. She embraces the man to whom she was once engaged. "We're here, can you believe it? What a horrible trip. We were stuck for five hours in the middle of nowhere while they cleared the tracks. Stuck in those cramped seats with a four-year-old whose idea of fun was running up and down the aisle to the water spigot and the bathroom. He tortured us. I slept maybe an hour in the last twenty-four."

"Well, come in, come in," Miles says, a bit flustered by the rush of her words. Ten years ago he nearly married this woman, but now he cannot imagine it. "You could use a drink, I'm sure."

"What I could use," Sylvia says, "is a shower followed by a bath followed by a long, long nap."

They move toward the front door, all except Alan, who—after paying the driver—still stands in the circular driveway next to the luggage, taking in the house and the hillside that slopes down in a series of terraces and gardens. "My god, Miles," he says. "My god, I never get over it. Your own little island, isn't it? You've got everything just the way you want it."

Their train was delayed, it turns out, by an accident; a log truck was broadsided by a freight train doing eighty miles an hour. Alan got the story from one of the stewards. The driver of the truck was drunk, and he had passed out on the crossing. Although two engineers were in critical condition due to the ensuing derailment, the driver, miraculously, was thrown clear, and rescue workers found him wandering in the forest. He was blind, his teeth had been knocked out, and his forehead wore a crease as though he had been struck by a baseball bat. He wept for the circumstances of his former life: his marriage, his mortgage, the child who needed braces, the mill owner who had refused the drivers a raise. The steward shook his head. "Poor son of a bitch is in for it now," he said. "He thought he was broadsided before. Just wait till they get through with him." He paused for a moment, considering. "Not that he should be parking a truck on the tracks, sabotaging trains, mind you."

The first flush of dawn appeared while the train sat motionless beneath them. Alan left for the washrooms to shave and brush his teeth. Fish was asleep next to Sylvia, whose eyes, although closed, were ringed with the blue shadows of sleeplessness. There would be hell to pay later. In the washroom, an elderly man was shaving with an electric razor. Burn marks traced his cheeks and jawline, while his throat sported a three-day growth of whiskers. The razor buzzed, and he sang, "Daisy, Daisy, give me your answer true . . ." in a voice that faltered like an adolescent boy's. Alan took the other sink, spreading out his shaving utensils: mug and brush, shaving soap, and straight razor. His face in the mirror looked pale and a little pasty, his eyes red, his hair limp. This trip on a stationary train was responsible for that. The day and night of a thousand miles seemed interminable; to be stuck was a penalty out of Dante. By himself the trip would have been manageable and not altogether uncomfortable; he would have spent the duration drinking and smoking in the club car. There might have been a cribbage player among the other single travelers. The time would have passed in an exchange of anecdotes, the delays met by jokes with the Southern Pacific as the punchline. With Sylvia along for the ride, and now Fish, those options were no longer available.

Ten years ago he had gone into Goldstein's, ostensibly for a pair of worsted slacks, and he had come out with his best friend's fiancée. *Why?* Why had he done that? It was a question for which he had no answer good enough, and all the bad answers were too bad to contemplate. He hadn't intended to defile the sanctity of friendship; he had fallen under the spell of romance; he had been jealous of such settled happiness; he had obeyed the dictates of his stars.

Whatever the cause, only a year after their marriage, he had begun to notice the women in his bank again. One of the tellers had invited him for a drink in her apartment, and her red hair and mushrooming chest had been inducement enough. Evidently the competition with Miles had been more important than the prize. What he had not counted on was that in winning Sylvia's hand and heart, he had also acquired her facility in spending money, which was at least the equal of his own. Bankruptcy was a constant thought.

Miles had done much better for himself in that respect— married to a shipyard heiress with an estate, a portfolio overflowing with liquid assets, and the attitude that money did not matter. Once again, he thought, Miles had achieved without intending to, as though possessed of some power that magically protected him from trouble—the castaway who always made it to shore.

Alan had nearly finished shaving when the train lurched under his feet and the mirror threatened to swallow him. He nicked the skin above the angle of his jawbone, and a drop of blood boiled in the opening and threatened to run down his neck. Stanching the flow with moistened toilet paper, he watched the mirror as the white dab at his jaw turned crimson, then black. Another five hours, barring anything else unforeseen, and they would be in the safe harbor of the Portland depot. He dried his hands and face and collected his shaving gear, then stepped into the corridor, where his steward had taken a position at the windows.

"Look." The steward held Alan's arm, drawing him closer to his own point of view. They were rolling slowly along the foot of a forested hill. Several small fires dotted the hillside. Freight cars lay on their sides like a child's toys. What was left of a log trailer was as twisted as a tin fork. The truck was black with char. "Man, oh man," the steward said. "How that poor son of a bitch got out alive is beyond me. He woulda been better off dead than the shitstorm that's coming, and you can bet he's going to get exactly what he deserves."

The wreckage slid by like flotsam, the train picking its

way through the tangled steel, and the thought occurred to Alan that everyone gets what he deserves, but almost no one gets what he might consider to be fair.

"There were pieces of that truck for a mile," Alan says, "freight cars like pick-up sticks, and one fire was no more than twenty yards from the tracks."

"We're just lucky our train wasn't the first one through this morning; otherwise we could've been killed," Sylvia says. She seems to enjoy the drama of saying this: "We could've been killed."

"How awful." Ariana visibly shudders. "I can't stand the thought of it."

"A disaster," Alan says. "No question."

The four adults are ensconced in the great room. Drinks have been poured, and Alan and Sylvia are getting the trip out of their system; they are enjoying the sensation of their own mortality having been preserved. Meanwhile, the children play. Freddy and Mira are introducing Fish to the many staircases in this old house. The servants' stairs between the kitchen and the cellar. The concealed stairwell built by bootleggers during Prohibition. At the top of the sweeping staircase that leads from the bedrooms to the great room, the children cluster, spying on their parents. Their presence is no secret, but the adults are wise enough to pretend otherwise. Soon enough their offspring tire of such boring conversation—*adults!*—and skulk away in favor of other pursuits. They settle for the basement stairs. Freddy finds the pull chain for the light bulb, and off they go—Freddy first, then Mira, then Fish—descending into the basement with its sweating cement walls and its odor of mildew, mouse droppings, and D-Con granules. Miles Lambert's workroom, formerly the coal cellar, is lined with box radios in various stages of repair. A portable phonograph sits on the workbench. Freddy picks a record and places it on the turntable. A soprano voice reaches a note that drives the children's hands to their ears and laughter into their throats. The basement lights are controlled by two switches, and Freddy finds the other pull chain. Off go the lights, and the darkness is complete.

"*È strano! È strano!*" shrieks the high, unearthly voice.

"Ah-ooh," moans Freddy.

"Ooo-hoo-hoo-hoo-hoo," Mira calls.

"Oh no, oh no, oh no, no, no, no, no," Fish whimpers, no irony or pretense intended.

The disembodied echoes bounce off the cement and reverberate throughout the house, and the adults listen, eyebrows cocked, to the strange sounds emanating from the floor beneath their feet.

For two years in college Miles and Alan were roommates, but their friendship survived mostly intact. Neither was particularly neat, but they were not so messy as to use shovels when they cleaned. Miles cooked the occasional meal; Alan did laundry once a week. They played squash together each Monday, Wednesday, and Friday afternoon, and almost every evening, when they could no longer study, they drank beer from quart bottles and played cribbage for a penny a point. If a dollar changed hands during the course of a week, it was rare. They did not call muggins on each other, and they did not replay let points unless the offending player made the call. They made an odd pair, in appearance as well as vocational interest: Miles the engineer, a bit unkempt, a gawky Abraham Lincoln scarecrow, all knobs, knees, and elbows; Alan the finance major, compact, with an Ivy League haircut and a penchant for blazers and flannels. But such differences did not matter where their friendship was concerned; they had known one another since first grade, and each knew the other as well as he knew himself.

Tonight, after bunking the children together dormitory-style in the third-floor bedroom, the wives also go to bed early, leaving the men to their own devices. The cribbage board is found and dusted off, bourbon is uncapped, and for old times' sake quart bottles of beer are retrieved from the refrigerator in the basement. They drink carefully now, these thirty-two-year-olds, for they are family men with wives and children and responsibilities; no more going to bed with a thick head at four in the morning. At midnight, after only four games, they stop in unison and call it a night, the bourbon nearly full, only one quart bottle drained.

"Goodnight, Alan," Miles says, shaking hands with his long-time friend.

"See you in the morning, you old skunk," Alan says.

They make plans for a squash match at dawn; they'll be up with the chickens, have their sweat in before breakfast and Bloody Marys with the sun.

"Even though I don't have my own personal court in the back yard, I'll have you know I've been practicing," Alan says. "I'll mop the floor with you, you old bag of bones, I'll have to give you ten points each game just to make it fair."

When they part, in front of the spare bedroom occupied by the Beckers, it is with that challenge, as well as the last twenty-five years, hanging in the air between them.

Sleep descends over the occupants of the house. Clocks tick, the old house creaks, boxsprings groan as first one, then another of the adults turns over.

Ariana, an uneasy sleeper at best, wakes with a start, conscious of having dreamed, but the dream itself is just out of reach. A tease. The radium dial of the bedside clock puts the early hour just shy of two o'clock. The house ought to be quiet, but a thumping, creaking noise, responsible for waking her, is coming from the third floor where the children have been deposited. She slips from bed, quietly puts on robe and slippers, and makes her way through the dark hallway to the east stairwell. What could it be? She runs through a list of possible causes, but there have been no mice for the past six months. The dog is outside. The toys might as well be alive. Now the noise is coming toward her! She can hardly restrain her imagination from the images found in ghost stories and her own dream life. Specters, wraiths, ectoplasmic horrors. But it turns out to be nothing. Only Fish. Coming down the stairs on his bottom. *Creak, thump, creak, thump.* She is about to say something when she realizes he is more asleep than awake. In the dim glow of moonlight his eyes appear glazed, unfocused, as though he is viewing something no one else can see. She takes his hand, thinking to lead him back to the third-floor bedroom, but guides him instead to Alan and Sylvia's room.

Frankly, she does not much care for her husband's friends; they strike her as chains from the past, a reminder of betrayal and disloyalty. That Miles seems to welcome their visits makes no sense to her. She has imagined pranks to enliven their stay: sand in the sheets, vinegar in the water pitcher, salt in the sugar bowl. Nothing really malicious but mischievous and discomfiting. Of course, she will never do any of the things that her imagination suggests unless Miles gives some sign of affirmation.

But now, at two o'clock in the morning, she can share her guests' own child with them, can't she? It's not such a terrible breach of hospitality, is it? She opens the Beckers' door and gently pushes Fish into the darkness of his parents' breathing. "Go on," she whispers, "get in bed with 'em. Get cozy." She closes the door behind the retreating child and then, her good deed accomplished for the night, heads downstairs to the kitchen for Irish coffee. Insomnia is a terrible thing, and she has it terribly; she welcomes nightmares as evidence of sleep. Any interruption at night and she will absorb the dark hours of early morning into her soul. But on this night the laws of probability are suspended. Ariana makes her coffee, an alchemist at her secret work, and then, after no more than two swallows, falls into deep sleep on the couch in the study. The reading lamp pools light in the depressions of her face. Two books lie face down on her chest: a sociological tract on utopian communities on her left breast and Sandburg's biography of Lincoln on the right.

So Ariana is unaware of the movement she has started: Fish stands by his mother's side of the bed until Sylvia awakens with a start and a prickle of fear of this face inches from her own.

"Goddamn it, Fish," Sylvia whispers through the pounding of her heart. "What are you doing here? Come on."

The boy turns but waits for his mother to lead the way. Sylvia, who is unfamiliar with the layout of the house, makes two circuits of the second-floor hallways before locating the door to the stairwell. Fish follows at the end of her hand.

"Come on," she says again. "Ups-a-daisy, back to bed with you." Fish obediently climbs the stairs, his mother at his back. Sylvia stumbles. Fish waits. Sylvia pushes him forward once more. "Go on. Back to bed, little man." Fish stands helplessly in the doorway until Sylvia climbs the last stairs, enters the bedroom with her son, and pulls back the covers. Mira and Freddy, mouth breathers, sleep the sleep of the charmed; they neither wake nor stir. Sylvia experiences the envy of age for youth, possibly for the first time. She tucks Fish into his bed, begins to leave, then turns back at the sound of his whimpering. It's a strange bed, a new environment, she thinks. After all, what can it hurt to keep the little guy company? She stretches out on the floor next to the bed. A few minutes, he'll fall asleep, she'll go back to her own room and an honest-to-god mattress.

Her breathing slows; an hour or more passes. When she does wake, her joints are stiff, her senses foggy from her nap on the wood floor. The children sleep undisturbed. *Kids.* Petty little tyrants. She gets to her feet unsteadily and staggers to the stairs, which she navigates slowly but successfully. In the second-floor hallways problems occur. Turn right or left? The doors are all the same and offer no clue. She becomes so disoriented that on her first try she goes back into the aquarium dark of the stairwell, tripping over the first step. On her second guess, the doorknob in front of her turns, and though the room is dark, she can tell that for once in her life she is as lucky as she is ever going to get. The left side of the bed is vacant; this must be the right room. Thank God she hasn't barged in on Miles and Ariana!

Miles feels the bed shift as Sylvia gets in. He turns to pull up the back of his wife's nightgown, and fits himself against his ex-fiancée. There they will stay in good-natured and comradely heat, spooning and snuggling and pressing themselves against each other, until a few minutes past five o'clock. When, in the light of a window facing the east, Sylvia notices that the long, pale fingers cradling her breast are not her husband's. "Oh, sweet Jesus," Sylvia says, alerting Miles.

"Sylvia? What are you doing here?"

She leaps away from the bed as though it were contagion itself. Her nightgown feels like a second, corrupted skin against the skin of her thighs.

"I went upstairs. I came back to my own room. How did this happen?" she says. Shock becomes embarrassment, which becomes self-accusation—that somehow this is her fault, that she has willed this game of musical beds. "Where's Ariana?" she says. "And why aren't you sleeping together?"

The bedroom is washed in orange light.

"I don't know," he says. "I don't know."

In the fifth game Alan hits the shot he has dreamed of all night long: a forehand drive that grazes the sidewall, hits the front an inch above the telltale, and dies in the back corner.

Miles drops his racquet. "Nicely done," he says. He can afford to be magnanimous; leading 12-5 in this final and deciding game, he has the match well in hand. Alan has not lied: his game is improved; he won the first two games and seemed in control of each rally's tempo. But in the next three games Miles turned away the slashing drives with well-placed returns, touch shots, finesse strokes. As power shot after power shot was turned away, Alan seemed to become desperate, as though the game meant something more than a workout. He broke one racquet against the back wall in frustration while

Miles looked away. There have been a few other unpleasant moments: during one ten-point span Alan hit Miles three times, twice on poorly played corner shots that seemed to be calculated more for the likelihood of hitting Miles than for their effectiveness. Red welts are even now rising on Miles's calves and behind one knee. Alan has disputed several serves, receiving as well as serving. But the worst came just a moment ago when Miles hit a pinch shot to the backhand side. From deep in the back court Alan called for a let, though he was clearly out of position and Miles was not an obstruction to the ball.

"You're sure?" Miles said.

"Yes, goddamnit, I'm sure. You've been camping in the center the whole game."

If I'm in the center, Miles thought, it's only because your shots left me there. But etiquette required a quick nod and a replay of the point. Which Alan won with his best shot of the match. Where's the justice in that? And he wins the next five points, bringing the final game to 12-10, but his forehead is buzzing and his legs ache. Precision deserts him. He drives a forehand into the telltale with a horrible clang and mishits Miles's next serve into the ceiling. On the final point Miles hits a gentle lob that drops along the back wall nearly on a vertical. Alan tries to scoop it out, but the shot is simply too much to handle, and the game, the match, is over. Alan throws his racquet against a sidewall, saying only "Son of a bitch" when the head flies off the neck. Miles opens the waist-high door, and they emerge from the court in silence. The sky is lead gray, overcast with sluggish summer clouds that promise humidity and oppressiveness. Their shirts and shorts are as soaked as if they have just walked out of the sea.

They strip and dive naked into the green water of the Lamberts' archaic, unrepaired, and unmaintained pool. Miles dives deep into the opaque water and experiences a momentary disorientation: Which is up and which down? When he breaks the surface Alan is already toweling off, a threadbare terry robe folded at his feet. Miles climbs the ladder, unsteady and fatigued, dries off, then shrugs on a black flannel robe decorated with eyes, a Christmas present from one of his off-center cousins. It could belong to either a magician or a housewife in Gresham.

"Your pool is a disgrace," Alan says. "A guy could kill himself in there and you'd be three months finding the body."

"Everything's old," Miles says. Alan is still smarting from the match, he knows. He chooses not to take offense. "It's getting older by the day and costs a fortune to redo. The house is giving us plenty to work on. It's a twenty-year birth."

Past the swimming pool and above the reflecting pool, Sylvia and Ariana wait in the gazebo. A table has been set, and a pitcher of Bloody Marys is waiting.

"Well, who's the hero?" Sylvia asks. She coughs smoke from her breakfast cigarette. Despite the warm early morning, she is wearing a sweater and hugging herself. A bracelet of large wooden beads clanks the table top each time she reaches for her glass.

"Not me." Alan tosses the pieces of his racquets into one corner of the gazebo and slumps into a lawn chair. "The big guy's too much. All those little dink shots ought to be illegal."

"Don't be a sorehead, Alan," Sylvia warns.

"I'm not being a sorehead. It's ugly squash, that's all I'm saying."

"It sounds sore." Sylvia holds out a Bloody Mary glass to

her husband. "You need one of these. If I drink any more I'll be loopy before seven." She turns to Miles and gives him a look that might be termed meaningful. "I'll be dancing on the table, you old skunk. I won't be responsible. I don't have Ariana's constitution."

Alan takes the glass. "I'm not sore."

Sylvia is not altogether certain of her memories from early this morning. When she opened the door to her room Alan was sitting on the side of the bed in his underwear, complaining of stomach pains, of a headache, of having slept like hell. Downstairs she found coffee already made and Ariana asleep on the couch in the study. She opened yesterday's *Oregonian*, but she looked over the top of the page at the other woman, who gradually awoke under the pressure of Sylvia's scrutiny. All of that she is sure of. What she cannot make clear are those hours before five when she knows she was in a bed not her own. It could have been a dream. A dream of a dream. When Alan and Miles made their way up the terraces to the gazebo, she wished they would vanish, leaving only their ghastly robes in twin puddles on the dewy grass.

Miles cannot even look at Sylvia. Ever since that moment when her voice broke into his consciousness, he has not been able to ignore the sense of her skin that lingers on his fingers and in his groin. The sense that ten years ago she could have ruined his life except that she and Alan conspired to save him. Knowing that, why does he still wish to be locked into a motel room with her, at least once? Just once.

"I think I'll take a peek at the children," Ariana says, "and then I'll do the eggs."

"I'll go with you," Sylvia says. "I'm freezing my ass off out here anyway."

The women leave, and the men are by themselves once more. In front of them the reflecting pool is a flat mirror, without a puff or the suggestion of a breeze to disturb the surface of the water. The clouds have hidden Mount Hood from view. The air smells gassy and saturated. Miles and Alan drink, then pour out more. They eat celery as though it were meditation.

"You're playing well," Miles offers. "Your drives are stronger than they were five years ago."

"No. You've still got the touch."

"You should come up for one of the club tournaments," Miles says. "You'd see how much your game has improved."

Alan bites off a stalk of celery. "Against a bunch of eighty-year-old doctors and overweight insurance salesmen? I don't think so. Besides, some of us have to work."

"Ah."

The clouds, so wet and heavy, now begin to leak—a drop or two at first, then a steady hemorrhage, the patter of rain maintaining a sleepy tempo on the gazebo roof. Miles pours out the last of the pitcher, and he and Alan drink without speaking, enclosed by the curtain of the rain. A second pitcher tilts in a bucket of ice. They make good progress; they welcome the spirits and bless the weather.

"You know," Alan finally says, "you could pay a little less attention to Sylvia, if you don't mind. She is my wife. *My* wife."

So there it is, finally. Ten years after the fact.

"Just because you can still beat me at squash doesn't mean you have the right to meddle with my family."

Alan as the guardian of morality.

Miles clears his throat as though to mount a defense. "I

am not meddling with your family, nor am I paying undue attention to Sylvia. She was *my* fiancée, but you married her. What's done is done."

"Is that right?"

"That's right."

"You're sure about that?"

"Absolutely, positively. I'm as sure about that as I'm sure that all your forehand needs is a deeper knee bend on your back leg."

"That so?"

"Here, let me show you." Miles gets up, a bit wobbly, and picks up one of Alan's amputated racquets. He assumes a ready position, then lunges forward with his left leg extended. "You see, you bend your left leg because you have to, but if you don't bend your right, it throws everything out of whack. You bend your back instead, your shoulders aren't square, you over- or undercompensate with your swing. Try it."

Alan shadows Miles, using Miles's racquet, stepping forward with the left leg, bending the right, but instead of a shadow swing, Alan brings the throat of the racquet down on the crown of Miles's head. The racquet splinters, the head snapping off this racquet as well, bouncing over the half wall of the gazebo and bringing Alan's total of broken racquets for the morning to three. Miles has gone down like a log.

"You goody-goody son of a bitch," Alan says, stooping over the taller man. "You and your goddamn know-it-all lessons. You think I didn't hear her voice in your bedroom this morning?"

The Beckers are packing to leave, four days earlier than expected. Their train leaves at five o'clock, and there are nine hours left to endure. Miles, after regaining consciousness, has withdrawn to his bed. At his request, Ariana brings up from the cellar the portable phonograph and the records so reverently slipjacketed, and now through the furnace vents comes the sound of strangled voices made more ghostly, more unearthly by the ductwork. The children race through the house moaning like banshees until Ariana points her finger to the french doors overlooking the back yard and tells them to find something else to do. Reluctantly, they troop outside in raingear, Freddy, then Mira, then Fish, like a little lost battalion. Sylvia is in the bedroom she could not find earlier this morning. Their suitcase is open on the bed, but she cannot make herself begin the tedious process of folding and stacking clothing that she took out only yesterday. The empty maw of the suitcase mocks her. Goddamn Alan. When did he get so temperamental all of a sudden? Over a stupid goddamn game, of all things.

At the moment Alan is just getting out of Miles's Buick in the train station parking lot to change the date on their return ticket. This morning's rain has continued unabated, and he runs across the parking lot hunched inside his jacket. A lost soul. He feels like a lost soul. His crimes are mounting. His oldest and dearest friend. First he stole Miles's fiancée, and now he's nearly killed him with a squash racquet. But he had reason. He had reason enough, he thinks, in Sylvia. Oh, Miles. They sat next to each other in every grade and every class. They were pals at school and at home; they played basketball together and took dance lessons together. At the spring cotillion they each danced with a one-legged girl, and their fascination with her wooden leg nearly started a feud between them. Maybe the fuel for conflict was inside them from the very start. And now he is the pariah, and Miles's scalp is split open from the top of his head to an inch above his right ear. The Lamberts' family physician came to the house to stitch him up, and Alan paid the bill, but he will not be through paying for this outburst, he knows, for quite some time. Long after Miles is restored.

At the moment, though, Miles cannot quite believe he will ever feel whole. His head throbs. Each stitch seems distinct in its pattern in his skin. On the phonograph, the record spins: Cio-Cio-San and Pinkerton sing their love duet. The inconstancy of Pinkerton! His assurances of love are more ironic than even Pinkerton—who is well meaning but as shallow as a drip pan—can guess. Miles plays the scene at the end of Act One again and again in spite of the pain at the base of his skull.

Ariana hears the duet repeat and repeat as she offers her help to Sylvia. The bittersweetness of such false assurances seeps under the doorway and through the adjoining wall. It will be fine with her to get these tiresome guests out of her house. Since the Bloody Marys at dawn, she has been nursing a bottle of bourbon, but there's only so much alcohol can accomplish. Sylvia's progress with the packing has gone no further than her own underwear and one pair of Alan's socks. She is crying as she rolls and unrolls the socks. "I never meant to hurt Miles," she says to Ariana as though hers was the hand on the squash racquet. "Never in a million years did I mean to hurt Miles. I wasn't leading him on, honest. It's just that one day Alan came into the shop with a fresh haircut, these white, white teeth, and clean fingernails, and I said to myself, 'Girl, this is what you need, this is what you deserve.' Now look at me."

The children play. Adults have different games that are impossible to understand. Freddy, Mira, and Fish play
follow-the-leader, hide-and-seek, and duck-duck-goose.
They run and shout and do barrel rolls down the hill through
the wet grass below the bedroom windows. They run laps
around the pool and its green, algae-laden waters. Ariana has
outfitted them with slickers and hats and boots; the rain is no
different for Freddy and Mira than the air they breathe. But
Fish fusses over the water that runs down his neck and col-
lects like cobwebs in his eyebrows. He has a fit when Freddy
and Mira run faster than his fat little legs will go. He stomps
his booted feet and throws his hat into the bushes. He fusses,
that is, until Mira pushes him into the shallow end of the
pool. She could take no more and meant to hear no more of
it. He grabs hold of the side and, like a spirit of outrage,
screams and screams and screams. Ariana, who must be
everywhere for everyone, comes running. Pulls the dripping
Fish from the water. Reprimands Mira and Freddy while sup-
pressing a wink. Marches them all back into the house, where
she serves them toasted cheese sandwiches and tomato soup
and tells them stories of the time between seconds, how in
those moments between breaths the soul experiences whole
lifetimes. She folds shirts for Sylvia, changes records for
Miles, offers bowls of strawberries to the children and a snack
to Alan when he returns. And then—*thank god!*—it is time for
the Beckers to go; the taxi is idling in the driveway, the bags
wait at the door. But where is Fish? Since their dessert of
strawberries the children have separated into solitary activities and no one has given much thought to his whereabouts
until, with a panic born of guilt, the adults check the green
water of the pool. Nothing. They search the gardens, the

bathhouse, and the squash court, calling, "Yoo hoo. Fish. Come out, Fish. Come out, come out wherever you are." Even Miles in his bathrobe and his blood-encrusted head wound. Still nothing. The cabbie is tapping his watch, the meter is running, and the Beckers have a train to catch. Freddy and Mira could tell them where to look, but now they are gone too. Hiding with Fish in the cellar with the lights off, where Fish crouches under the workbench with its array of gutted and dismembered radios. He shields his eyes from the darkness and wishes desperately, desperately to stay and not to go.

8
EVERY
THIRD
THOUGHT

Without his presence Mr. Lambert's cellar workroom seemed oddly uninhabited. There was the usual clutter: wires, vacuum tubes, and sockets. The radios on the bench were in the same state of disrepair as they had been when I came downstairs five days earlier except that a slightly thicker layer of dust now coated the exposed tubes and coils. But nothing familiar remained in the windowless room. Some scent had vanished from the air.

I found the boxed set of records where Mira told me to look. Mr. Lambert's ancient collection of *Madama Butterfly*. By now it was antique, the box was disintegrating, and the vinyl records were scratched, the sound quality poor at best. There were other, newer versions shelved in the study. Callas, Tebaldi, Victoria de los Angeles. But he had loved the Toti Dal Monte version best. When he listened to Dal Monte sing *"Un bel dì"* I believe he left his body in a way that Mira, who claimed to have experience in such matters, did not entirely appreciate. I never got the attraction. Not at all. Not really. Occasionally a note or two would seem to promise something, a hint, a whisper. But then whatever it was would be gone, and I'd be left with Italian that not even Italians could understand. Mr. Lambert had only smiled when I told him I didn't get it, that it was just a bunch of fat people torturing themselves and others. He told me we'd get around to my opera education in due course. He had taught me several other things over the course of the summer: he corrected the flaw in my forehand, he explained the principles of radar as it was used in weather forecasting, and he tried to give me an idea of why—when they had plenty of money—he and his wife didn't spend it all at once. I looked at his ancient Buick, the pool with the broken filter, and I couldn't help but wonder.

Mrs. Lambert was the one who wanted the records. Mr. Lingenfelter needed to make a tape before the service. He didn't want any fussing around, trying to place the phonograph needle in just the right groove. I had volunteered to go back to the house because I felt very much the outsider just then; I thought it might be good to get away from Mira and Freddy and all their relatives who had flown in during the last couple of days. Mr. Lambert's parents, a couple of his doddering aunts, a dozen cousins or more, all in well-pressed, serviceable fabrics. They were nice enough, but their sincerity, like their luggage, was everywhere, and I was glad for the excuse to get away. What I hadn't counted on was feeling spooked by the house. Each room had its own presence and kept me turning to look over my shoulder. There was movement always at the corners of my eyes, and I kept hearing music just beyond the edge of sound. Only the workroom in the cellar felt empty, but by the time I made it downstairs I was thoroughly unnerved. If the lights had gone out, I would have wet myself. I ran up the cellar steps as though pursued and nearly made it to the front door before the phone rang. Even then, I almost chose to ignore it.

"Yes," I said, panting a little, "Lambert residence."

"Fish? That you, Fish? I'm having a tough time hearing a goddamn thing with all this racket." My father's voice crackled, broke apart, faded, then erupted again in the receiver. "They're tearing up the concourse right in front of the goddamn phones. Can you believe that?" The sounds of jackhammers and power saws threatened to overwhelm whatever he said next. Something about home. I got that much.

"Dad," I shouted, "what? What did you say? Where are you?"

"LaGuardia. New York. We're back on American soil, kid, and boy, let me tell you it feels all kinds of good. Your mother and I are going to spend a couple days here fooling around, and then we'll fly out to get you. Okay?"

"No." I swallowed hard. "No, you've got to come now. Tomorrow at the latest. Mr. Lambert died, he had a stroke, he was supposed to be okay, but then he wasn't, and now the funeral's Friday. Dad, did you hear me? Dad?"

The night before Mr. Lambert died, Freddy and Mira were at the hospital with their mother until the close of visiting hours. Afterward they went to Rose's for cinnamon rolls and coffee. Mrs. Lambert figured that on a Friday night they could all use a break. Mira called me from the hospital to ask if I wanted anything. A sandwich, some pastry, a slice of German chocolate cake, a torte, a tart, whatever. The cinnamon rolls were enormous, she said, and would have looked at home on a giant's plate. When the phone rang, however, I had been entangled with Amanda Baird on the sofa in the study, and I told Mira I wasn't that hungry. Amanda's shirt was off, but she was not making it so easy with her bra, the mechanics of which—after two months of practice—I had yet to figure out.

"I really think he's going to be okay," Mira said. "The doctors and nurses, everyone is pretty optimistic. It looks like I was being silly last week. Too much mysticism, too little science, I guess."

"If you have to feel stupid about something, at least it's a good something," I said. I was holding the phone in the alcove so I could look back into the study. Amanda was stretched full length on the couch. The fingers of her right hand were splayed across her brown stomach, which reflected the light from the desk lamp nearby. "That's really good news about your dad. You guys have a good time, you deserve a little fun."

"We'll give it a shot. Mom says we should be home around eleven, so not to worry."

"I won't."

"You're sure we can't get anything for you?"

"No," I said, "I'm fine. Really. I'll watch TV or go to bed early. I'll read a book. Don't worry about me."

"Well, don't do anything too ambitious."

We said our goodbyes, and Amanda sat up on the sofa.

"All's well in Cleaverville?"

"I guess. They're going to Rose's and eat their worries away. Mira said her dad seems better."

"How nice for them." Her lip curled, then relaxed. "Rose's, I mean. I'm glad about Mr. Lambert."

I was glad too, but there were Amanda's recalcitrant bra and her jeans, which I thought might be coaxed a little lower.

It had been a summer-long ritual, as tightly choreographed as a geisha's dance. On our first meeting at the river she had clearly defined the boundaries as well as the movements: all clothing above the waist was subject to removal, the anatomy available for handling, while everything below—apparel as well as parts—was locked as carefully as a bank vault for the weekend. I had hoped that tonight might be different. But so far I had nothing other than a swollen upper lip—from the sort of kissing performed only by enthusiastic amateurs and those wearing braces. *At last!* With the hooks finally free, the cups loosened around her small breasts, the straps slid down her arms, and a rush of warmth went straight to my groin.

There had been a month or more when we stopped seeing each other. But after Mr. Lambert's stroke, Amanda came to the door with a macaroni casserole for the family and forgiveness for me, and we resumed as though there had been no interruption.

I kissed her neck and shoulders, her nipples and her tummy, and her fingers were in my hair, pushing and pulling my head, guiding my mouth to its next destination. But the moment my fingers snaked inside her jeans and fiddled with the elastic of her panties, she slugged me on the side of the head so hard I lost the hearing in that ear.

"Jesus," I gasped. "Are you nuts?" My ear was ringing and felt twice its normal size. "I think I'm deaf."

"I said no," she said. As though I might not understand otherwise, she spoke slowly and clearly into the ear that still worked. "No means no. Don't be a shit. We've been through this before," she added, as though weary of repeating a lesson for the umpteenth time.

"I thought tonight would be different."

"It wasn't, was it? And tomorrow won't be any different either." She slipped the bra straps back over her shoulders, re-hooked herself, and pushed her arms through the sleeves of her shirt. "I have to go anyway. I'll see you tomorrow, and maybe you'll remember your manners, you monster."

Then she was out the door, refusing my offer to walk her home. The walk was downhill, the way was dark, but she preferred solitude. I watched her brown figure disappear into the shadows at the end of the driveway, and as I stood on the front porch the summer night came alive as though laughing at my immaturity and inexperience. Crickets performed their one song. Stars glittered in the black sky like mica. A sudden, unexpected breeze ruffled the trees, the trunks and branches creaking like masts under full sail. The breeze carried other sounds aloft as well. The clatter of a trash can as it tipped onto its side, then rolled along the sidewalk in the wind. An engine turning over. The laugh track from a television. From the direction of the Catholic cemetery came the sound of several voices singing—or attempting to sing—"Row, Row, Row Your Boat." Their concern seemed to be for volume rather than tune as they sang the round. *Life is but a dream. Merrily, row.* What were they doing? Who would sing in a cemetery on a dark night? Whose dream was I?

I went to my room on the second floor, got into bed, and watched the hands of the clock mark the passing of the hours. I tried to remember the feel of Amanda's breasts in my hands. At ten-thirty the rottweiler at the bottom of the hill began to bark and strain against its tether. At five minutes after eleven a car chugged past the house, its glasspacks throbbing like a death sentence, and at eleven-fifteen Freddy and Mira and Mrs. Lambert came home. They locked the doors, said their goodnights, and then two doors on the second-floor hallway closed: Freddy and Mrs. Lambert going to bed. I heard Mira's footsteps in the stairwell, then the door to her room on the third floor likewise closed.

I closed my eyes. I swear I only closed them, but when I opened them again, Mira was sitting on the edge of my bed, shaking me.

"I'm worried," she whispered.

"What?"

"I need you to help me." She had brought her Ouija board downstairs. I hated the thing, and Mira knew it. "Please?"

"Christ, Mira, I was actually asleep. Asleep."

"I know, I'm sorry. You looked sweet. I wouldn't ask if it wasn't important."

We sat on the bed in our pajamas, cross-legged so our knees touched. Mira had a penlight that she propped up so we could see the old board in the dark room.

"I keep seeing a fire around his head and chest," Mira said. "The doctor says he's doing fine, he keeps talking about Dad's excellent recovery, but I'm still getting a bad feeling. Either Dad's in real trouble or I'm going wacky."

She breathed deeply a time or two as though she were about to dive off a three-meter board, then put her fingers on the pointer.

"Madame Claudia, are you ready for us?" Mira said. The pointer trembled under our fingertips. The first time she had asked me to play this game with her, I thought she was moving the pointer herself, a parlor trick, a dumb party stunt, but I didn't think so anymore. And now when the pointer moved, I couldn't help but shiver.

"Madame Claudia?"

The pointer swept across the board to *YES*.

"I need to know the truth. Is my dad getting better?"

The pointer circled the board before it returned to the word *YES*.

"See, Mira," I said. "Just your imagination."

"We'll see," Mira said. "I don't always trust what I see. Either way. It's too easy to influence what you see." She turned her attention back to the Ouija board. "When will he get out of the hospital?"

The pointer began to spell out an answer: *T-O-M-O-R-R-O-W*.

"Can you believe that?" I said. "Tomorrow. That's great, Mira."

"I don't believe it," she muttered. "He looked like hell when we were with him tonight. He still can't talk right or move his fingers."

"Maybe he'll go to a nursing home until he can build up his strength."

"Maybe." She bit her lower lip. "Madame Claudia, is he going to a nursing home from the hospital?"

The pointer moved—almost reluctantly, I thought—to *NO*.

"Is he going to come home?" I asked.

The pointer edged away, then returned to *NO*.

"Well, where is he going to go?" Mira asked.

We watched as the pointer spelled the letters *H-E-R-E*, but Mira wasn't waiting for anything more. She threw the board against the wall and the pointer out the open window. The penlight rolled under the bed.

"Stupid shit," she said. "I don't know why I'm such a

sucker for this stuff." Then she threw her arms around my neck and began to sob so that her whole body shuddered. The bed shook beneath us.

"Don't worry," I said. "I'm sure it'll be all right."

I suppose if I had been Freddy, standing in the open doorway of a dark, shadowed room, watching his younger sister being embraced by a summer-long house guest on top of an unmade bed, I might have come to the same conclusions. He pulled me away from Mira and hit me so hard I thought my eye had popped free from its socket. I had a sudden fright that my eyeball might be down on the floor along with the penlight and the dustballs. My nose mushroomed blood.

"Don't you ever," he said. "I better not catch you again."

He had set me up with Amanda just so this moment would *not* happen, but—in his mind—it had happened anyway.

"Freddy, you idiot!" Mira murmured, sotto voce.

Freddy did not stick around for explanations or apologies. He had a date with Gale Lewis, and no doubt the two of them would be rolling around in the quack grass near the river soon enough. Fortunately for Freddy, she had no older brother. He went through the window, and we heard his angry footsteps along the joints of the roof.

Mira guided me to the bathroom. In the mirror, the face staring back at me was covered in blood. Both sides of my nose were still gushing, and blood dripped from my upper lip like a waterfall. Bright red drops splashed against the porcelain. But that wasn't the worst of it.

"Hoo, boy, you're going to have one doozy of a shiner," Mira said.

The skin underneath my eye was already turning the color of burgundy. My eye still felt as though it had been shoved into the wrong place. It made a poor fit. I turned the cold tap, ducked my head into the sink, and watched as the water swirled red.

"I'll go get some ice."

"Okay."

Mira went downstairs to the kitchen. Evidently her mother was also downstairs, unable to sleep, because both of them came to the doorway of the bathroom, Mira holding a towel full of ice cubes. Mrs. Lambert had a drink in her hand, but when she saw me she put it down on the counter and tilted my head back.

"I don't think anything's broken," she said. "Your nose might be a little puffy in the morning. Mira has some ice for that eye."

"I'm fine," I said, hoping I wouldn't begin to tear up. "Surprised more than anything."

"Freddy ought to be put on a leash, Mom. I don't know what the big ape was thinking."

Mrs. Lambert was blotting water and a few stray drops of blood from my face. "Does anyone?" she said. "Does anyone know what anyone else is thinking?"

"You know what I mean."

Mrs. Lambert pinched the bridge of my nose, then rolled small squares of toilet paper and pushed them into each nostril. I held the towel against the side of my face.

"Your pajamas ought to be washed and probably your bedding as well." Mrs. Lambert sighed and touched my cheek with the palm of her hand. "I'm sorry, Fish. We're not such good hosts sometimes. I'll go strip the bed. Mira, why don't you pop some popcorn while Fish puts on some fresh night-clothes? See if you can find an old movie on television. Something we can laugh at. Especially if it wasn't meant to be funny."

And that's how we were when the phone call came from the hospital: Mrs. Lambert, Mira, and I eating popcorn and watching as Steve McQueen fought a blob of alien goo. Mrs. Lambert worked on her bourbon, Mira read one of her theosophy tracts while she watched, and I held a cold, wet towel to my face as the ice melted. The phone rang a little after one in the morning, and the three of us froze in the bluish-gray light of the television set and in the midst of our own thoughts, our own fears. Mrs. Lambert would confess later that she had been more worried about Freddy—about his absence—than about Miles. So not only did she have to cope with Mr. Lambert's sudden and unexpected death, she also had to accommodate the guilt that it wasn't her husband about whom she had been thinking. For some reason Mira was convinced that Claudia Montoya-Jones was calling from the grave, reproaching her for discarding a legacy in a moment of anger. She knew the idea was absurd, but she couldn't shake it, especially since the Ouija board had been vindicated in this most unhappy manner. I just hoped it wasn't some new dire announcement from my parents: that not only were they getting divorced but neither wished to have custody of their son. We each had a fear that the ringing phone signalled, and as a result we each committed a cardinal breach of loyalty without even realizing it: neither were we present when Miles Lambert suffered his fatal heart attack, nor were we thinking of him.

Freddy was not home, of course, and he too would feel guilty in the days and weeks to come. He didn't come home for more than a day, so he didn't know about his father's death until funeral preparations were well under way.

Even through the noise of the machinery, I heard the sound of my father choking back tears, then the sound of the phone dropping. My mother picked up the receiver, and it was her coughing I heard next.

"What's this all about, Fish? What did you say to your father?"

"Mr. Lambert died."

"Miles Lambert is as healthy as a horse. That's a horrible, sick joke. What are you trying to pull?"

"It's not a joke, Mom. He's dead. The funeral's the day after tomorrow. You've got to get here."

And then I outlined the same story I had told my father.

When the call came from the hospital that Mr. Lambert had died, I was as devastated as Mira and Mrs. Lambert. I thought I would cave in on myself. But when I spoke to my father, I realized I knew something he did not: I knew that his best friend from childhood had died. I knew it and he didn't. I knew all the details firsthand, and in that information was the power to punish my parents. For cheating on one another. For using money instead of love. For being gone while I was here. For failing to fix what had broken between them. I hated the news I had to bear, and I hated myself, but I enjoyed the leverage that knowledge provided. I enjoyed it too much. The waiting rooms, the doctors, the hours I had spent in the hospital with Mira and Freddy and Mrs. Lambert. How the stroke had left Mr. Lambert unable to speak except for a garble of nonsense, the line of his mouth twisted into an unintended snarl. How he had begun to regain the use of his right arm and leg. How we had all begun to relax, hoping that the worst was behind him. How we had been eating popcorn and watching *The Blob*. And then how a heart attack had killed him.

Even knowing that each new detail caused new pain, I rattled on and on, unable to stop, until my father dropped the phone. And then, after my mother took over, I could barely speak at all. I didn't have the stomach for it. For anything beyond a recitation of the facts.

"Okay," my mother breathed, "we're coming. We'll get our tickets straightened out, then we'll get the hell out of here. Okay? That sound okay to you?"

"Sure, I guess so."

"Ah, shit," my mother said, and from the sound of her voice I thought maybe she had begun to weep as well. "I can hardly believe it. He was such—he was such a sturdy sort of man. He always made me feel as though everything was under control. I thought he'd live forever. I'm sorry, this has been a pretty lousy summer for you, I know, and I wish there was something I could do to make it up to you."

"It's been okay."

"Your father and I—well, I wrote you a letter. I never write letters, so you know it was important."

"I got it."

"I'm so sorry. I've never been so sorry about anything my whole life."

"Okay, Mom. I know you guys haven't been happy."

"No, that's true enough. But that's not your fault. Listen, your father wants back on the line. I'll see you as soon as we can get there. Give Ariana my sympathies and a hug, will you?"

In my haste to get the *Butterfly* records I had left the Lamberts' front door wide open, and while I waited for my father to reclaim the phone, I suddenly became aware that the smell of high summer was pouring through: the yeasty odor of the front lawn, newly mown; the sun-heated stones of the driveway; the heavy, humid air that invited one to part it like a curtain. Grass sprouted in the mortar between the cobblestones. Nature never stopped trying to reclaim its own. In Los Angeles, I knew, the temperature would be hovering near one hundred. Had I been there, I would have been invited to pool parties and barbecues at the homes of friends. There would be the usual crowd of guys and here and there a few girls from school looking self-conscious in new swimsuits and tanning lotion. A couple of the mothers and most of the fathers would get drunk, and after the smoke cleared from the grill and night was gathering, one of the boys would push one of the girls into the pool, and then everyone, including the adults, would cannonball into the water. Waves would slosh over the sides and onto the cement, trickling finally into the flowerbeds with their bird of paradise, camellia, and star of jasmine bushes, date palms, and oleander. The scent of chlorine would rise and permeate the air. I could have scripted an entire evening, though it didn't seem possible that such things were still done.

"Fish, you still there?" My father's voice brought me back. The box of records sat next to the telephone, the corners held together with masking tape. "Fish?"

"Yes, I'm here."

"We'll make it to the funeral, okay?"

"I know Mrs. Lambert would appreciate it. Mr. Lambert's relatives are here, and they're driving everyone nuts."

"We'll get there as soon as we can. Maybe tomorrow morning. Tomorrow afternoon at the latest. We won't leave you stranded."

"I believe you, Dad. Really. You don't have to harp."

"Okay. I'm just a little overcome, you know? Did I ever tell you that Miles Lambert once pulled me into our dormitory window using three sheets tied together? Pulled me up two stories after curfew. He was wiry and strong and a good, good friend. Even when I wasn't."

The funeral for Miles Lambert was held in the Lambert house at two o'clock that Friday afternoon. My parents did not arrive in Portland on Thursday, as they had promised—there were problems with reworking their tickets—but after a series of flights that stopped in Chicago, Minneapolis, and Seattle, they did reach the house at lunchtime the day of the funeral. In the middle of the night they spent six hours in Seattle, trying to sleep on benches. Through a fluke all of their luggage was routed onto a plane headed for Phoenix, so they showed up empty-handed at the front door. Mrs. Lambert had to pay cab fare because they had used all their cash on airline liquor, and all their travelers' checks were zipped up in my mother's toiletry bag. They had been in airplanes or in airports for twenty hours, they were beat, and they had no clothes but the shorts and sandals and tee shirts they had worn since they left New York. But then, I wasn't one to talk. In the week since Freddy punched me, my cheek and the skin around my eye had turned purple and various shades of green and yellow. Mira said I was wearing camouflage.

By the time my parents arrived, Mira and I were already dressed for the service and were killing time in the kitchen, looking at all the casseroles, cakes, and pies that friends of the family had brought over that morning.

"Hey, Sport," my mother said. "Nice shiner. You run into a door or what?"

"Hi, Mom." We faced each other from opposite sides of the kitchen island.

"Well, do I have to beg for a hug?" Her tone was sharp, and her grip was fierce. "My god, you've grown six inches this summer," she said at last, holding me at arm's length.

Mrs. Lambert pushed the swinging door open. She held a sundress on a hanger. "All I have that might fit is this one, Sylvia. I could never wear this, it comes down to my ankles."

My mother took the dress, her eyes vacant. "Thanks. I'll be fine. Your father," she said to me, "is upstairs trying to find something to wear other than a tee shirt from the Eiffel Tower. My guess is he'd appreciate a hello."

"Okay."

I climbed the main staircase from the great room. I had been waiting all summer for this moment, but it had arrived in a form entirely different from what I had imagined. The stairs seemed endless and as steep as a ladder. My father was in the last room off the hallway, Mr. and Mrs. Lambert's bedroom. He stood in their walk-in closet wearing one of Mr. Lambert's gray suits without a shirt. The sleeves were at least three inches too long, and the pants would have had to be cuffed to his calves in order not to drag the ground. I was staring, and he caught me. Swimming in the coat and pants, he looked like a child wearing his father's clothes; he did not have the advantage of looking adorable, however. He needed a haircut, his complexion was creased and crossed by the marks of fatigue, and his jaw was stubbled with whiskers.

"This is ridiculous," he said, looking at his reflection in the full-length mirror at the back of the closet. "I knew it wouldn't work. I just didn't want to hurt Ariana's feelings."

"Don't you feel a bit weird, wearing Mr. Lambert's clothes?"

My father began rifling the chest of drawers on Mr. Lambert's side of the closet. "You know the damn airline lost all our damn luggage. I could've cried." He flipped through the hangers. "Maybe a pair of jeans would work."

"Maybe. Or a pair of sweats?"

"Another possibility." He went back to the chest and opened drawers he had already looked in once. "You've talked to your mother?"

"I saw her downstairs."

"Did she say anything about our plans once we get home?"

"No," I said. "She didn't say a thing."

"We've got a couple surprises I think you'll be glad about."

"Does this mean you've figured out which one of you I'll be living with?" Another consideration suddenly presented itself. "Or are you sending me away to boarding school? Not a military school. Not with all those phony uniforms and ranks."

He laughed as though I'd said something funny. "No. Nothing like that. We'll tell you when we have a chance to sit down together. So," he said, sizing me up for the first time, "who punched you out? You look like a damaged raccoon."

"Freddy," I said, "by mistake."

"You patch things up?"

"Not really. We've managed to avoid each other for a week."

"Well," he mused, "I hit poor Miles over the head with a squash racquet once. Not by mistake. I wanted to kill him. We talked over the phone all the time, but I never saw him again. The biggest mistake of my life."

He held my chin in one hand, tilted my cheek to get a better look at the bruising around my eye. "Freddy was just providing a little family balance, I guess."

"The next time you hit someone," I said, "tell me when I need to duck."

Mr. Lingenfelter, the funeral director, had a problem at the last minute, so the service did not quite come off as scheduled. The tape he had made of selections from *Madama Butterfly* broke when he was threading the reel-to-reel. He tried to splice the tape together, but he didn't have time to do a first-rate job, and there was evidently something wrong with the tension on the heads. The tape broke a second time in another spot, and then it broke on the first splice. He threw up his hands. "I'm sorry, Ariana, I don't know what's wrong with this machine. I tested it this morning and it worked. It worked perfectly." He was a fussy man with an immaculate manicure and an ulcer, and it was clear that this change in plans would cause him pain for a week.

"That's fine," Mrs. Lambert said. "We'll use the phonograph. That was more Miles's style anyway. He probably wouldn't have recognized the music if it weren't distorted."

We were seated outside on the back lawn facing the patio. Mr. Lingenfelter had arrived early that morning to set up chairs in the spongy grass. An easel holding Mr. Lambert's portrait stood on the patio along with the casket. My parents and I sat in the second row. My mother wore Mrs. Lambert's sundress; my father had found a pair of Freddy's slacks that nearly fit and one of Mr. Lambert's summer shirts that was at least one size too large, but he was presentable if not particularly stylish. There must have been a hundred or more people sitting in folding chairs. They waited patiently while Mr. Lingenfelter grew more and more flushed with each new crisis of the tape. A young, rather confused Episcopalian minister stood in the center of the patio, waiting for the signal to begin.

Finally, after Freddy went downstairs for the phonograph and Mr. Lingenfelter found the approximate spots on the records, Mrs. Lambert said, "Okay, Father Walter. I believe we're ready at last."

The young man opened his prayer book. "'I am the resurrection and the life, saith the Lord: he that believeth in me, though he were dead, yet shall he live and whosoever liveth and believeth in me, shall never die.

"'I know that my redeemer liveth, and that he shall stand at the latter day upon the earth: and though this body be destroyed, yet shall I see God: whom I shall see for myself, and mine eyes shall behold, and not as a stranger.

"'We brought nothing into this world, and it is certain we can carry nothing out. The Lord gave, and the Lord hath taken away; blessed be the name of the Lord.'"

Father Walter cleared his throat. "In committing our brother Miles Lambert to Almighty God, we shall, at this point, depart from the usual order of service. At the family's request we will listen to several musical interludes and reminiscences from family and friends."

Mrs. Lambert rose from her seat in the front row. Her dress was black, but she was dry-eyed and matter-of-fact.

"Some of you were here twenty years ago when Miles and I were married." She looked at my mother and father, and I thought I saw the ghost of a smile. "You sat in folding chairs on this very lawn. But instead of sunshine, you wore navy surplus ponchos in a steady rainstorm. Here we are again. Miles is dead. I can't tell you what a shock that is to me. We met in Samoa. He was stationed on the island and as lonely as can be; I had run away from my mother, and one place was as good as another. We were both anxious to love and be loved. He promised that he would never leave me, and I believed him, and when we fell in love Puccini's geisha girl was present to mark each stage in our courtship and marriage. All right, Mr. Lingenfelter."

The funeral director had cued up "*Un bel dì*," and the music started slowly, then increased in pitch until it arrived at the proper speed. Toti Dal Monte sang Butterfly's fervid dream. She was convinced that one fine day her husband's ship would sail into the harbor, that he would come for her, that he would call to her, that he would become concerned for her safety while she hid—just for a moment, just to tease him—from his sight. This much I knew from Mr. Lambert. Sitting in the folding chairs, we followed the translated libretto that Mrs. Lambert had thought to enclose in the announcement of the service, and just for a second, while the voice soared through the scratches and the lousy phonograph, I thought I might begin to cry. But then Butterfly began to sing "*Chi sarà, chi sarà . . . chi sarà, chi sarà . . . chi sarà, chi sarà . . .*" until Mr. Lingenfelter bumped the needle into the next groove.

When the aria was over, one individual after another rose, walked to the patio, and said a few words in affirmation of Mr. Lambert's goodness and virtue. He was a straight shooter in business, a magician when it came to getting people together; he was generous with his time, an affable host, able to orchestrate complicated entertainments easily and without fuss. He enabled others to see themselves. This went on for a good forty minutes or more. Mr. Lambert's parents spoke; they were proud of their son. Freddy said he would miss his father, even his lectures and the chores he assigned as punishments. Mira, so recently reassured in her spirituality, said the dead were not really dead; they dwelt among us and then came back in new forms, so she was sure to meet another incarnation of her father at some point in her life. The minister was cringing, so she laid it on thick.

Mrs. Lambert turned to me. "Fish? Anything you want to say?"

"I wish I could have spent more time with him," I said. "He taught me a lot already this summer, but there was lots more I don't understand." I took a quick peek at my parents, who were sitting attentively, holding hands. "He taught me about the sun, the moon, and the stars, their astronomical names and how radar works, but he was going to teach me about opera. I don't see how anybody could like it, but he had his reasons. Since the beginning of the summer, I think I heard most of the stories, but what good will that do? He's not around to tell me what's important."

Then Mrs. Lambert looked at my parents. "Sylvia? Alan? Did you wish to say anything? Sylvia and Alan," she said to the rest of those sitting in the folding chairs, "were two of Miles's closest friends. They grew up together, and in spite of horrendous difficulties, they spent all day yesterday and this morning on crowded airplanes just to be here with us."

My father and mother stood in their borrowed clothes. "Miles Lambert," my mother said, "was like goodness and mercy to me. Even when Alan and I announced our engagement, he wished us only the best. I don't think there was a mean or jealous bone in his body. He turned rainstorms into parties."

"We were so close," my father said, the instant my mother stopped speaking, "I married his fiancée. I suppose that sounds kind of funny, but it's the truth. Miles Lambert was like a brother to me, and when his mind was on other things I stole his girl. I loved him like a brother, and now and again we fought like brothers. For the last ten years or so, it was easier to be on good terms by staying a thousand miles away from each other and talking occasionally on the phone, but that doesn't change the fact that we loved each other, the way you can love certain pains because they let you know you're alive. With Miles Lambert gone, I won't know whether or not I'm breathing."

My parents sat down; everyone had at last run out of things to say. Mr. Lingenfelter played two other selections from the recordings that had been shelved in the study: *"Chi il bel sogno"* from *La Rondine* and *"O mio babbino caro"* from *Gianni Schicchi*. After these pieces, Mrs. Lambert rose once more.

"I haven't said much about what Miles's death means to me. When I first met him, his life meant I didn't have to kowtow to my mother over anything anymore. We got married, and I exchanged subservience to my mother for allegiance to my husband. It may sound rather heartless, but Miles's death means that for the first time in my life, I'm free. It means I can issue my own orders. But what a terrible price! Such a terrible burden! To have one's freedom for a life that no longer *is* a life. He called me his free spirit, and now he's let me go. But for what? The center doesn't hold forever. Am I supposed to fly underground? When he was alive, my every third thought was of Miles Lambert. Tonight, as I get ready for bed and the sleep that never comes, I'll probably wonder if I was ever married or if I ever loved."

Mr. Lingenfelter played two more selections then, both of which came from *Madama Butterfly*: the love duet between Pinkerton and Butterfly followed by *"Che tua madre."* In the latter selection, Butterfly, no longer able to believe in the illusion of her marriage, asks what will become of herself and her child. Will she resort to begging? What will become of them? Death would be preferable to the dishonor of being abandoned by her husband-lover.

When the last notes died away, Mrs. Lambert stood on the patio, facing us all. "Okay. That's it. We're done. Thank you one and all. Thank you for coming, but I'm not sure I could take anymore. There's food in the kitchen if you're hungry. Please take with you whatever you brought, since none of it appeals to me. Frankly, I'm not sure I'll ever eat again."

Father Walter began to recite a benediction, but Mrs. Lambert cut him off before he was halfway through.

"I think that's just fine, Father. We need no more of that, thank you. Thank you very much."

She left the patio, firmly closing the french doors behind her. Mira and Freddy shook hands with the bewildered minister in front of the casket while Mr. Lingenfelter began to fold the chairs as quickly as those sitting in them stood up.

I heard murmurs from several of the business types, one of whom said that Mrs. Lambert was always half in the bag, no matter the time of day or night. In the row behind us, a woman wearing a fox stole said to no one in particular, "Well, wasn't that the strangest thing!"

My parents' news was what I had hoped to hear all summer long: they had decided not to get divorced after all. While they were thirty thousand feet over South Dakota, my mother had agreed that it would be too much trouble to start over again. The trouble of learning to live alone or even with someone new was just too much to contemplate, she said, sighing. It was a capricious choice, but then so was marriage. To which my father nodded.

And then there was Miles Lambert. The matter of his death, that is. Without either of my parents saying so, I got the feeling that the death of my mother's first fiancé and my father's oldest friend had changed the way they could view their lives. They had only each other now as a telescope into the past, as a mirror of the person each had been. When Miles Lambert died, they lost a separate vantage point from which to see themselves, and divorce was no longer an option they could easily afford.

9

THIS
OTHER
LIFE

My parents intended to leave the day after Mr. Lambert's funeral. What with Mr. Lambert's relatives, Mrs. Lambert did not need additional houseguest or guests who stayed in a hotel and then quietly reminded one of how considerate they were. She had plenty of those. Enough was enough. She needed guests who left.

On Friday, the day they had arrived, my father had purchased three tickets for a flight leaving Portland Saturday afternoon. We were not going to be an additional burden, my father said. Not if we could help it.

But opposition to that plan came from an unlikely source: Mrs. Lambert. She met my parents in the great room while my father was dialing the cab company for the ride to the airport. My parents' luggage—and their travelers' checks—still had not arrived, but there was money waiting at the Western Union counter.

"You're not leaving," Mrs. Lambert said. "That's not possible."

"We couldn't possibly impose any further," my mother said. "Not with all these people in the house."

Then, as though to punctuate her remark, Mr. Lambert's mother entered the great room holding an empty mayonnaise jar, a rubber spatula rattling inside. "Dear?"

"Downstairs pantry," Mrs. Lambert told her mother-in-law.

"You see?" said my mother.

"See what?"

"Ariana," my father said, "if we thought we could make things any easier for you, we'd stay. But at this point I think the better part of courtesy would be a quiet departure."

"Geez, Alan," my mother said, "get down off the high horse, why don't you?"

Mrs. Lambert pressed her fingers against her temples. "Okay, I admit it's been hard. I think Miles had about a jillion relatives, all deaf, and none with a sense of the obvious. So what? You haven't come for ten years. Then you leave after a day?"

I stood next to my suitcase, holding the pointer for Mira's Ouija board. After her father died, she had looked in the flowerbeds below her window, but just as it seemed to have a life of its own when it was tracing answers on the board, it had disappeared and was nowhere to be found. Until that morning we were to leave, when I saw it floating in the green water of the swimming pool. How it had gotten there, two hundred yards from the house, was a mystery. A dog maybe. But that seemed pretty far-fetched. I had hoped to see Mira so I could give it to her, but she hadn't been home all day, and neither Freddy nor her mother had a clue to her whereabouts. But she had a theatrical sense of timing, and she chose that moment to open the front door. She took one look at my parents and me, my father's old suitcase, and she began

to wail, "Mom, you said they were going to stay! You told me
we could go to the island one last time! Fish and me."

She saw the pointer in my hand. "You found it! I looked
everywhere. You probably had it all along."

"I didn't know they were going to leave so soon," Mrs.
Lambert said. "It's not my fault. I've been trying to change
their minds, but your father's friends are as pigheaded as he
was. They think they're some sort of burden and that they
know what's best."

There was more of the same, back and forth, and in the
end a compromise of sorts was arranged. My parents would fly
back to Los Angeles because, after spending a summer over-
seas, they had more than a few financial matters to attend to,
bills to pay, accounts to juggle. But I would be allowed another
week. I was not another intruding guest, Mrs. Lambert
claimed. In fact, I was insurance that her own children
wouldn't become a nuisance while she waited for the last of the
relatives to leave. I don't how much of it she herself believed,
but I was grateful for the sentiment; as much as I had looked
forward to going home all summer long, I now also realized,
with the force of a blow, how much I had hoped to stay.

My desire to stay at the Lamberts' was real, but so was my
wish for home, all of it complicated by Amanda Baird. That
morning, while my parents slept late, recovering from their
recent spate of airports and off-hour flights, I had walked
downhill to her house. I had never before gone all the way to
the front door; we usually met at the river, and when I walked
her home she rarely let me get closer than the corner of her
block. But I had not seen her since the night Mr. Lambert
died, none of her family had attended the funeral, and I

thought this might be my last chance. I tried the doorbell, which didn't work, then knocked on the door. A flicker of movement at the living room curtains, then the quick sound of footsteps and the scraping of a deadbolt before the door opened and Amanda slipped out and grabbed my hand.

"Come on," she said. "Don't ask questions. I don't think he knows I left, but you can never tell."

She started to run toward the river, and I followed. We waited for a break in the traffic on Macadam and then began to run again, letting the slope of the hill carry us down to the straggle of beach.

"There," she said, laughing. She hugged me hard and kissed me with a ferocity that I hadn't experienced in any of our marathon sessions. "You made it with fifteen minutes to spare. I had a letter ready in case you didn't show, but I had a feeling."

From behind a tree she pulled a backpack, a sleeping bag, and a square white envelope with my name on the front.

"I wrote this last night while cranky Frank was at work. You want it?"

"What's going on? You leaving or something?"

"You are one quick study, Fish Becker. You bet I'm leaving. I'm getting my sweet ass out of here." She consulted her watch. "In ten more minutes. Duncan said it shouldn't be a problem with the car."

Her sister, Sheila, and Duncan Rhodes were coming to take her to the ashram where Amanda and Sheila's mother was living. Sheila was going to stay at the Rhodes' house; they had offered her a basement room, but if things got too tense living in the same neighborhood as their father, she might go to southern Oregon as well. It had all been worked out. They could both use a change of scene, Amanda said, but first she needed a clean getaway. Frank, their father, had turned weird, weirder than normal, walking naked through the house after his shower and talking about purging the world of Satan while looking meaningfully at Sheila and Amanda, as though Satan's work involved the character of women.

"He goes to work every day and he comes home. He hasn't done anything certifiable that I know of, but it's scarier than hell. I keep waiting for the explosion. But no more."

"Jesus," I said, "he's a fruitcake. But running away. You sure you know what you're doing?"

"You're going home, right?" I nodded. "And your parents are back together. That's what Freddy told Sheila. So don't ask me whether I'm sure. I'm not sure about anything. All I know is I'm not hopping a freight and it's not white slavery. I'm going to see my mother, for god's sake. Mom's nutty, but she's not dangerous. Not that I know of."

"But you hate brown rice."

"Yeah," she said, laughing, "many parts of the pine tree are edible. The cuisine's liable to be awful." She sat down on the sand and patted the spot beside her. "By my watch we've got four minutes of kissing time left. I know that Freddy set us up to keep you away from his sister, but it's been okay, this summer, don't you think? So long as your hands stay where they're supposed to."

Duncan and Sheila were not as punctual as Amanda, so four minutes turned into more than an hour, but we did not relax our hold of each other or catch our breath until we heard the sound of a car creeping toward the guardrail above our heads. Duncan and Sheila in his father's red Impala. "One last smooch," she said, then handed me the envelope. "Mom's address is inside. You can write me. Or not."

We climbed the embankment and threw Amanda's sleeping bag and backpack into the Impala's trunk. Duncan cracked a joke about lip lock. Sheila said they needed to move it. Amanda opened the back door. "Wish me luck," she said.

"Luck. Lots of it."

She waved, and then they were gone. Duncan pulled out with a spray of gravel, and when I reached Macadam, they were already out of sight.

A month later, the school year well under way, I wrote Amanda at the address she had given me. Two months after that, the letter came back marked "no such address." I called Duncan Rhodes, but he and Sheila had broken up not long after Labor Day; she had moved out of the basement, and he wasn't sure where she had gone. She wasn't in school, so she might have gone to the ashram. But you never knew with those places. Those swamis, he said, hair today, goon tomorrow. Ha, ha.

My parents left that afternoon. My father gave me a bear hug and my mother kissed me while Mira watched from the front door.

"We'll change your ticket," my father said, "and you can pick it up at the Continental counter. By the time you get home, we should have everything back to normal. We'll go see a game or two before the season's over. And then there's the Rams. We'll go to the Coliseum and see a Rams game."

"Okay."

"And Fish," my mother said, "you need to let me know

what you want to do about your birthday. You want a party, ideas about presents, you know the drill. I don't suppose you want a set of lederhosen, do you?"

A week after my flight home, I would turn fifteen. "No thanks," I said. "You can keep the leather shorts."

"Nuts," she said. "I would have been all set. Oh well. You think about it and let me know, okay?"

"I will."

"All right. We're going. Be good, Fish. Be a help to Ariana." She slid across the back seat of the taxi, and my father got in beside her.

"Don't do anything, I wouldn't do," he said.

"That leaves me a lot of room," I said.

"We'll see you next week at the airport."

"Okay."

Everyone was leaving, and if someone had offered me a ride to Bakersfield or Nantucket, I would have taken it.

"Ooh," Mira whispered in my ear. The taxi's brake lights flickered at the bottom of the drive. "A birthday. I just love a good birthday."

Midway through that last week, the phone rang while Mira and I were watching television. "Let's Make a Deal" was on, and we were both pretending to be interested in the contestants, the prizes, and Monty Hall. It was the middle of the day and the sun was shining, but neither of us felt like moving. "Never take door number two," Mira was saying to the young couple dressed like Raggedy Ann and Andy. "These guys have donkey written all over them." Then the phone rang. She answered it there in the study, and then she covered the mouthpiece with one hand. "Mom," she called through the open window into the garden, "telephone. It's Mr. Lingenfelter."

"Coming." Mrs. Lambert was pruning the roses. She stripped off her gloves, and somehow—by the time she came inside—she had found a glass of bourbon. Mira held the phone out to her mother, and Mrs. Lambert said, "What's the little fussbudget want now?"

Mira shrugged. She had told me that since the funeral Mr. Lingenfelter had been calling her mother every day. Sometimes twice in the same day. She wondered whether the funeral director's attentions toward her mother might not be romantic in nature. An opportunist with an eye toward the youngish widow. It was a possibility that made Mira's eyebrows arch whenever she spoke of the fastidious little man and her abstracted mother. But when Mrs. Lambert took the phone, her manner was pleasant and confidential. "Yes, Robert?" she said and winked. Five minutes later the Raggedy couple were the proud owners of a donkey and Mrs. Lambert's expression had turned somber. "I'm going to have to go over there," she said. "He doesn't have anyone else working today. If he left to come over here, the parlor would be empty. Wouldn't that just give you the creeps. You two can come along if you want, but 'Let's Make a Deal' doesn't come along every hour."

Mr. Lambert's ashes were ready. Normally Mr. Lingenfelter delivered the container personally, but today he was the only one in the store, and naturally . . . Mrs. Lambert found her purse while Mira and I put on our shoes.

An hour later we drove up the bumpy cobblestones of the driveway while Mira clutched a shoebox-sized container in her lap. Her father's remains were gray and as coarse as a workingman's beach. "I can't believe this, Mom. Couldn't he give you an urn or something? This is lousy."

"Your father wouldn't mind so much. We have the stone next to mother's. Robert's display vases cost a fortune, and I have something that will do just as well at home."

"He might as well have used a pickle jar. It's sick."

"Your father," Mrs. Lambert said, stopping the car and looking into the back seat at her daughter, "is not in that box. You, of all people, ought to understand that."

"Yes, ma'am."

Mr. Lambert had once requested—jokingly, Mrs. Lambert assured me—that his remains be scattered to the wind simultaneously by sky divers above Civic Stadium, Lloyd Center, and the Crown-Zellerbach paper mill, but Mrs. Lambert had told him he could forget that. The way she talked about his request, I almost wondered if they had had a conversation recently. Mira wanted to pour the ashes into the Multnomah Channel from the houseboat at Sauvie Island, Mrs. Lambert thought they should stay in a vase, and Freddy said they ought to be buried along with the radios and the opera records. For the moment, however, the shoebox was placed on the mantel above the fireplace, and Mrs. Lambert, Mira, and Freddy did not discuss it again in my hearing.

Two mornings before I was scheduled to leave, Freddy pulled out the chair across from me at the breakfast table. His job with the construction crew had ended the week his father went into the hospital, and except for his nightly exit through my window and rendezvous with Gale Lewis he was loafing until the start of school. It was the closest thing to grief that he knew. "Hey, Fishbait," he said, "how about a little squash?"

"I don't think so."

"Come on. Probably our last chance before you leave."

"Freddy," I said. "Freddy Freddy Freddy. I am not that big a putz, believe it or not."

"Listen," he said, "I'm sorry about popping you the other night. It was a mistake. I know that now." He touched the top of my head in a mock blow. "You're a quick healer, at any rate."

"Thank you, no. No squash." My right cheekbone still felt bruised and tender, but he was right about one thing: the purples and greens of my black eye had faded to the color of soot.

"One match, best of five. I'll spot you five points. No, wait. Make it seven. Seven points a game."

Once again I hadn't been able to sleep, and although I had stayed in bed as long as I could, I was still the first one up. The kitchen was cold; Indian summer would run for another month, Mira said, but already there was a tang in the air suggestive of fall. I ate cold cereal and read Carner's biography of Puccini. It had been Mr. Lambert's recommendation. I didn't have the discipline to read it straight through, however. I skipped the discussion of the maestro's illustrious ancestry, his childhood and student days, and headed straight for the meat. The La Scala premiere of *Butterfly* was a scandal, ruined possibly by a "well organized claque, hired by Puccini's enemies . . ." and the opera was not performed again until some three months later in a revised form.

"Seven points. I'm giving games away, Fishbait."

I closed the book on Puccini's greatest disappointment. "Okay, Freddy. Seven points. I suppose you can humiliate me as well as beat me."

"Don't be so negative."

In three months I had won only one best-of-five match straight up, and that on a morning when Freddy was still drunk from the night before. When he was fit he could have given me thirteen points each game and three points on a five-point tie-break, and he still would have won easily. Over the course of the summer my game had improved, but I was still light years behind Freddy, whose motive for playing me was a mystery. I was not a challenge.

In the first two games there was nothing different to report: Freddy won 15-8 and 15-9; I must have hit five forehands into the tell-tale during the first game alone while Freddy's drive shots died in the back corners and his pinch shots and crosscourts were geometric marvels of angle and line. I couldn't return his lob serve with any consistency.

"You ought to work a little harder," Freddy said at the end of the second game. I was dripping with sweat and my lungs burned, but I held out my racquet for the ball and the serve. The hard black ball felt like a rock in my hand.

He returned my serve easily, transforming my attempt at a lob into a backhand drive that scorched the sidewall. I stretched, but the ball was past me before I had even begun to move.

On his serve, I managed to push a lob return that skimmed the sidewall and dropped into the corner. Freddy hit a soft backhand crosscourt that bounced deep into the forehand corner, but I had time to see the ball and view the court. Freddy had cheated to the forehand side of the "T," but there was still room enough to hit a drive down the forehand wall. His legs were in my line of sight, though. They flashed like temptation, and I drove a forehand as hard as I was able into the back of his right leg, the ball burying itself in the soft skin directly behind the hinge of his knee. I might as well have shot him as quickly as he went down, as much as he began to howl. It was my best stroke, my best shot of the summer.

"You little piece of shit," he said, rocking on the floor, holding the back of his leg, which had already swollen to softball-sized proportions. The welt would eventually spread around his calf, a bracelet of internal bleeding. "I gave you the lane."

"I wanted a crosscourt," I said. "My point, 8-1."

"Fuck it," he said, a pained laugh seeping between his lips. "I'm through for the day, in case you couldn't tell."

"Fine. My match." I threw my racquet against the front wall and watched it splinter along the laminations of the head. For good measure, I beat his against the back wall until the head broke off at the neck.

"You little prick." Still laughing. "You want more racquets to bust up, there's some in the bathhouse."

"Asshole."

I was about to pick up the handle of his racquet, thinking that I could brain him, finish him off for good. Which was when he smiled at me, saying softly, "Okay, Fishbait, it's cool. What goes around comes around. We're even now, I think. How about you?"

During those last two weeks at the Lamberts' I had not been able to figure Mrs. Lambert out. Her husband had died, her house was overrun with relatives and friends, and the busybody funeral director was trying to put the make on her. But she didn't seem any different to me than she had at the beginning of the summer. She never seemed entirely aware of what was occurring in the time and space she inhabited; her eyes were locked onto some unfocused middle distance only she could see. Her drinking was the same, no more, no less. I can't say I ever saw her drunk, but she was never entirely sober either. She still gardened and mowed the lawn at whatever odd hour she took the notion. I had expected that following Mr. Lambert's death, some sort of change would come over her. That she might cry, for instance. But my parents and I had cried more over the phone when I first told them the news.

One night not long after my parents left, I found myself at loose ends. Freddy was out, Mira was in her room reading, and there was nothing interesting on television. I went into the dark study, turned on one of the pole lamps, and began skimming sections of the Puccini biography, only gradually becoming aware that I was not alone in the room. Mrs. Lambert was sitting in the leather armchair near the window, her face framed by the shadows cast by the lamp and the stacks of books on the library table in the center of the room.

"Mrs. Lambert," I said, so startled by her presence that I stood up. But then I was instantly regretful—what if she had been asleep and I had awakened her?

"Oh, Fish," she said. "It's you." I couldn't tell if her tone was surprised or disappointed.

"I'm sorry, Mrs. Lambert, I didn't know you were in here. I'm sorry if I woke you up. I guess I was just surprised."

"I wasn't asleep, but I suppose I was dreaming." Her mouth compressed itself into a smile, but her eyes were still lost in the faraway. "Miles was telling me we would have to do something together. Really together, he said. So it must have been a dream. But I would have liked to know what we would have done."

"Yes, ma'am."

"Don't worry, Fish. I'm not losing it. I know Miles is dead. I knew it the moment I came to myself and saw you standing there. Actually, I knew it before then. When Miles said we would do something together, I knew. I didn't want to believe it, but I knew. The notion of two people together, not just two individuals moving in roughly the same direction—it's impossible. As impossible as unicorns. A nice enough idea, but just as fantastic. What you will learn, Fish, is this: we're locked inside our own skulls, and every activity is essentially solitary. Playing games together. Driving in a car. Watching a movie. Intimate activities—conversation, even lovemaking. It's a dance, and both partners are so afraid of making a mis- step, they are so concerned about themselves, that they never even remember the color of the other person's eyes. Your par- ents, for instance; they're doing the best they can, but even after twenty years they can no more share a thought than they can share each other's skin. Don't blame them for it. Even Juliet didn't know what Romeo was thinking. And as for Butterfly," she said, noticing the book in front of me for the first time, "little Cio-Cio-San never had a clue."

The night before I was to leave, Mira, Freddy, and Mrs. Lam- bert threw a little surprise party for me even though my birthday wasn't for another week. Mrs. Lambert bought an entire German chocolate cake from Rose's, which would have fed twenty additional guests. By this time, however, Mrs. Lambert's in-laws had departed, and the cake bulked on the kitchen counter like a monument. Mrs. Lambert broiled steaks and baked potatoes, we had the cake and vanilla ice cream for dessert, and afterward they brought out presents, none of which was wrapped. Freddy gave me a brand new Seamco, a beautiful, well-balanced racquet that felt light as a feather in my hand. Mrs. Lambert gave me a new copy of the Puccini biography and, as a joke, a glass of warm milk. The milk had never helped her either, she said, although everyone recommended it. Good humor seemed to be, if not the cure, the only means of survival.

When her turn came, Mira seemed flustered. "I didn't know what to get you, Fish."

"Don't worry about it. You don't have to give me any-thing."

"No, no. I found something, but it's not new, and I don't want you to think I was just being cheap." She handed me an old five-by-seven, the colors of which had faded to weak pas-tels. It was a copy of a photograph I had seen often enough in my parents' bedroom on their dresser—my parents' wed-ding portrait. My father's arm was around my mother's waist, while my mother held a bouquet of roses and daisies. The long tunnel of the future lay before them. They were smiling. On the back of the stiff photographer's paper was an inscrip-tion in my mother's handwriting: "To Miles, with fondness and regrets, all our love, Alan and Sylvia, 11/7/48."

"I found it in the back of that old Philco Dad fixed last winter," Mira said. "He kept it with that picture of him and your mom. It's yours, it ought to be yours."

"Thanks." My parents, so full of their own lives, stared back at me. They seemed so young, yet so certain of them-selves.

"Speech," Mrs. Lambert said. "What's a birthday celebra-tion without a speech?"

"Yeah, speech," Mira said. "Come on, birthday boy."

"I don't know what to say," I said. "I really don't. Mrs. Lambert, Freddy, Mira—thanks for letting me stay here. I'm sorry I clogged up your whole summer. But I don't know what I would have done or what my parents would have done otherwise." The gifts lay on the table in front of me, each item a reminder. "I'm just so sorry about Mr. Lambert. I can't stand it. He knew so much."

Mrs. Lambert patted my hand when, despite my best intentions, I began to cry. I kept seeing him hunched over his workbench in the cellar, tubes and coils scattered before him—the inanimate objects that, when arranged by his hands, produced sound and life and heat. "There, there, sweetheart," she said. "It's not that much different than before. It's not as though we don't ever talk."

"It's just tougher to have a conversation," Mira said, "over that long a distance."

Mrs. Lambert said it was a special night. So she let us dip into the liquor cabinet. "It's your choice," she said. "You're adults. Or nearly so. And you're going to need the practice. Of choosing, that is." An hour later she was outside mowing the back lawn, the beam of the lawn mower's headlight sweeping back and forth, while Freddy and I sampled some of the better stuff.

"Don't be stupid," Mira said. She had swirled maybe an ounce of Jack Daniels in a fruit juice glass, smelled it, and declared it wretched. "I've heard stories," she said to me, "of people who fly with hangovers. When they get above twenty thousand feet, their ears start to bleed."

"They don't," I said.

"It's the truth."

"Mira," Freddy said, "you are full of shit."

"And their tongues swell up the size of a meatloaf."

"Cut it out."

"There are known cases of winos whose eyeballs popped right out of their sockets when they got to altitude. Go ahead, take a chance. See if I care."

My father always said that the best hangover cure was four aspirin before going to bed. Never wait until morning, was his motto. If you were going to be drunk, you needed to give the cure a little head start. When Mira huffed upstairs, I tried to think where the Lamberts' medicine cabinet might be. I didn't believe a word she said, but then again, some precautionary measures were not totally out of line.

Freddy and I played cribbage while we drank the Jack Daniels. Our fathers had played the game once upon a time. My father had taught me the rules and told me stories about the games he and Mr. Lambert had played, the memorable hands and the late nights. We played now and then, but I could always tell he didn't really enjoy it.

"I guess it isn't the same," I said, "playing with me. He would have preferred playing with your dad."

"They drank beer, smoked cigars, and talked about nookie," Freddy said. "It's hard to do that with a kid."

"I guess."

Freddy wiped me out four games running. He called muggins on me at least five times. The more bourbon we drank, the tougher time I had seeing all the fifteens, the various combinations, as well as the proper counting of the pairs. When we played the hands, he pegged on nearly every card until I could take no more. I would have thrown the cards in his face, but what good would that have done? I had almost broken his leg with a squash ball, he had given me a birthday present, and he was still an asshole. Every time I threatened to quit, he poured more bourbon in my glass. I finally staggered upstairs, pitched forward onto the bed, and closed my eyes until the room stopped spinning. I forgot completely about the aspirin.

It must have been a bad night for Mrs. Lambert and her insomnia because the back-and-forth growl of the lawn mower never seemed to stop, louder, then quieter, then louder again. The noise was so insistent, I wondered why the dead in all three cemeteries didn't rise up in protest at this disturbance of their rest.

When the lawn mower finally ceased, Freddy came through my room, pinched me on the butt, and whispered, "See you later, you little pussy. Don't let your ears bleed tomorrow, okay?" Then he opened the window, and out he went. I heard him tramp across the roof and then the ivy shaking on the trellis as he made his way down. He must have slipped near the bottom because I heard a thud against the side of the house, and I got up just in time to see him limping down the margins of the back lawn. He scuttled down the slope like the mad doctor's assistant, all arms and back, his legs threatening to collapse beneath him.

I dreamed so many odd things! Such a busy night! Lost at sea at the height of a storm, thrown about by winds, buffeted by rain and hail and snow, visited by spirits who sang a melody without notes, marooned, orphaned, abandoned. Alone. In the dream I was frightened, certainly, but not terrified.

Mira woke me. "Jesus, Fish, I heard you on the third floor. What's the matter with you?"

"Nothing. I didn't mean to wake you."

"Forget it. It doesn't matter anyhow. Let's get this show on the road. It's your last night, remember?"

"What now?" She had her backpack and the Ouija board at the ready. "Not the cemetery again," I yawned. "Not that."

"No. The island. We've got things to do."

"How're we getting there? Your mother driving us?"

She twirled a key ring around her index finger. "No," she said, "we take the Buick. It'll be like having Dads with us."

"Do you remember that first day at the airport?" Mira yelled. "I thought you had just climbed out of a hole in the ground." The Buick rattled and groaned, and conversation was difficult except at an extremely high volume.

Mira had never returned her father's keys. The day he had his stroke, she threw the keys into her backpack, and a week later there was no one to give them to. When we first opened the doors of the Buick, I wondered if this was such a good idea. Just my luck, I thought, twelve hours before going home, to die in an ancient automobile driven by a girl two years younger than the legal age. I had to admit, however, that given the empty roadways of two o'clock in the morning, her driving had become quite good.

"You looked like you just woke up," Mira continued, "and we were your worst nightmare come to life."

Her backpack was loaded—Mira had several items on her agenda—and as it turned out, her father was with us in more than the symbolic presence of the car. She had scooped part of his ashes into a Dixie cup, covering it with a piece of wax paper and a rubber band. Evidently, she had somehow talked Father Walter out of one of his prayer books because once we reached the island, our first task took us to the roof of the houseboat, where she turned to the prayer designated for the burial of the dead at sea: "'Unto Almighty God,'" she intoned, "'we commend the soul of my father, and we commit his body to the deep; in sure and certain hope of the Resurrection unto eternal life, through our Lord Jesus Christ; at whose coming in glorious majesty to judge the world, the sea shall give up her dead; and the corruptible bodies of those who sleep in him shall be changed, and made like unto his glorious body; according to the mighty working whereby he is able to sub-due all things unto himself.'"

She had a flashlight with her to read by, and when she turned the Dixie cup over, the ashes caught the light and sparkled in the darkness. A magic powder spinning in the air, then turning to dust on the surface of the slough.

"Bye, Dads," Mira said. Her cheeks were wet.

We watched the dark water drift by. It was a balmy night, and the air was still. A bright half-moon watched us with its lazy eye, the silhouette of its dark side quite visible.

"So what's the story?" I asked. "I thought you theoso-phists were pretty gung-ho on reincarnation."

"Oh, sure," she said. "Reincarnation makes more sense, don't you think? One day when I'm eighty, I'll see a baby in a stroller, and I'll wonder if his soul hasn't found another home. But we're flexible, you know? A little of this, a little of that. Besides, Dads always liked the Seabury prayer book, and even though he didn't go very often, he liked those Episco-palian high services, the incense, the bells, the fancy vestments; he liked the hocus-pocus in all of it. I did it for him."

She had a couple dozen candles in her backpack along with the cup that had contained her father, the flashlight, the prayer book, the Ouija board, and the pointer. She had forgotten matches or a lighter, though, so we were stuck with the flashlight. It didn't seem to matter. Mira invoked the name of Madame Claudia, and she was off and running. She had a ton of questions; for that matter, so did I.

"Madame Claudia, are you alone?" Mira began.

The pointer slid to *NO* under our fingers.

"Is my father there with you?"

YES.

"Can he speak with us?"

NO.

"Why not?"

The pointer began to spell: *N-E-W*.

"He's too newly changed, is that what you're saying? Too new across the border?"

YES.

"Mira," I said, "your mom said something about talking with him. How come she can and you can't?"

"My mom," she said, "has her own kind of life."

We asked Madame Claudia many things, not all of which she was able or willing to answer. Madame Claudia had no trouble providing answers to questions regarding school, future careers, and our favorite hobbies and interests, but about less personal matters she could be less than forthcoming, as elliptical as a fortune cookie or a horoscope. When we asked who was going to win the election, for instance, Nixon or Humphrey, the pointer moved to the word *YES* as though it were a yes-or-no question.

Other questions were just too far in the future, it seemed.

When we asked who we were each going to marry, the pointer froze entirely. Mira said that sometimes happened; she thought it might be a response to questions that shouldn't be answered. And such was the case when I asked about my parents.

"Will they stay married?" I asked.

NO.

"Will they get divorced?"

The pointer refused to budge. Not even when I tried to nudge it experimentally. Anxiety clutched my throat. "Is one of them going to die?"

E-V-E-N-T-U-A-L-L-Y.

Eventually, of course, was the answer to most of our questions. And eventually Mira bade Madame Claudia good night and switched off the flashlight so that we were once again alone with the dark night sky, the light of the stars, and the lazy eye of the half-moon.

"You tired?" Mira asked.

"I'm beat," I said, "totally beat."

"Me too. I could use a little nap right about now."

"That sounds okay."

I guessed that my flight home would be leaving in less than six hours. There was time. We lay down side by side on the plywood roof of the houseboat. Mira kissed me on the cheek. "You turned out okay, Fish."

I yawned. "You too, Mira, even if you are the weirdest girl I ever met."

And then we fell asleep, holding hands, her long fingers braided with mine.

When I woke, she was gone. My first thought was that as a practical joke she had driven home. *Wouldn't I be surprised?* But the Buick was still nose forward in the parking slip, a dark bulge, humpbacked as a whale, in the watery predawn light. At the edge of the roof was a puddle of her clothing, her shorts, tee shirt, bra, panties, and sandals. She had taken it all off and was treading the water, no more than fifty feet away. The splash as she jumped into the channel had been enough to yank me into this other life. The sun rose above Mount Hood, and the sky was flooded with its orange light.

She swept her hair away from her eyes. "Hey, Fish," she called, seeing me, "it's lovely, don't you think? A lovely day."